MY NEST OF SILENCE

My Nest of Silence

WRITTEN AND ILLUSTRATED BY

MATT FAULKNER

Atheneum Books for Young Readers
NEW YORK LONDON TORONTO SYDNEY NEW DELHI

ATHENEUM BOOKS FOR YOUNG READERS • An imprint of Simon & Schuster Children's Publishing Division • 1230 Avenue of the Americas, New York, New York 10020 • This book is a work of fiction. Any references to historical events, real people, or real places are used fictitiously. Other names, characters, places, and events are products of the author's imagination, and any resemblance to actual events or places or persons, living or dead, is entirely coincidental. • For information about special discounts for bulk purchases, please contact Simon & Schuster Special Sales at 1-866-506-1949 or business@simonandschuster.com. • The Simon & Schuster Speakers Bureau can bring authors to your live event. For more information or to book an event, contact the Simon & Schuster Speakers Bureau at 1-866-248-3049 or visit our website at www.simonspeakers.com. • The text for this book was set in Tiempos Text. • The illustrations for this book were rendered in Procreate on an iPad Pro. • Manufactured in the United States of America • 0922 FFG • First Edition • 10 9 8 7 6 5 4 3 2 1 • Library of Congress Cataloging-in-Publication Data • Names: Faulkner, Matt, author, illustrator. • Title: My nest of silence / Matt Faulkner ; illustrated by Matt Faulkner. • Description: First edition. | New York : Atheneum Books for Young Readers, [2022] | Audience: Ages 8 to 12. | Summary: A graphic novel/prose hybrid which tells the story of a young Japanese American man who leaves his family in the Manzanar internment camp to fight in the European theater during World War II, and of his ten-year-old sister who, frustrated over her brother risking his life for the government that imprisoned them, decides to stop talking until he returns. • Identifiers: LCCN 2020044386 | ISBN 9781534477629 (hardcover) | ISBN 9781534477643 (ebook) • Subjects: LCSH: Japanese Americans—Evacuation and relocation, 1942-1945—Juvenile fiction. | Manzanar War Relocation Center—Juvenile fiction. | World War, 1939-1945—Juvenile fiction. | Graphic novels. | CYAC: Graphic novels. | Japanese Americans—Evacuation and relocation, 1942-1945—Fiction. | Manzanar War Relocation Center—Fiction. | World War, 1939-1945—Fiction. | Japanese Americans—Fiction. | Selective mutism—Fiction. • Classification: LCC PZ7.7.F39 My 2022 | DDC [Fic]—dc23 • LC record available at https://lccn.loc.gov/2020044386

Dedicated to the memory
of
Robert Bly and
Malidoma Patrice Somé

And for my wife, *Kris*
Always

BEFORE we go any further, you should know a few things:

1. After Japan bombed Pearl Harbor, the US government took me away from my home, my school, and my friends and stuck me and my family in a prison camp in the desert just because we're Japanese American.

2. Now that my brother, Mak, has turned eighteen, he's signed up for the army, and they're sending him off to war.

3. I've stopped talking for the duration of the war. Or at least until Mak comes home.

4. My father thinks I'm abnormal.
I'm not.
Mama says I have an overdeveloped imagination.
But that just makes me exceptional.
Not abnormal.

MANZANAR RELOCATION CENTER
APRIL 1944

I'M GLAD THEY DIDN'T TEAR IT DOWN WHEN THEY STOPPED MAKING CAMOUFLAGE.
PROBABLY BE MORE WORK TO TEAR IT DOWN THAN TO LEAVE IT UP.
ALSO, THEY MIGHT WANNA USE IT FOR SOMETHING ELSE.
SOMETHING ELSE?

LIKE MAYBE A WAREHOUSE...
MAK. DON'T!

...TO STORE NOOGIES FOR YOUR NOGGIN WHEN I'M NOT AROUND.
CUT IT OUT, MAK!

LIKE WHAT?
OH, I DUNNO...

I KNEW YOU WERE GONNA DO THAT, YOU BIG JERK!
SUCH FOUL LANGUAGE! I'M GONNA TELL POP!

NOOGIES CAN CAUSE BRAIN BRUISES, Y'KNOW! YOU COULD STUNT MY GROWTH!
OH, CALM DOWN. YOU POURED WATER UP MY NOSE WHILE I WAS ASLEEP LAST WEEK. CONSIDER US EVEN.

FINE.
BUT YOU'RE STILL A BIG JERK.
WHATEVER YOU SAY.
C'MON, KABOCHA-HEAD. LET'S GO DRAW.
LOOKS KINDA LIKE A CHURCH IN HERE, DOESN'T IT? LIKE THAT CATHEDRAL IN SAN FRANCISCO.
IT'S SO PRETTY.
SO, WHAT'RE YOU GONNA DRAW?
NONE OF YOUR BUSINESS. THIS IS A COMPETITION. BEST DRAWING WINS. YOU PROMISED.
YEP. THE LOSER FOLDS THE WINNER'S LAUNDRY FOR A WEEK.

OKAY.
ON YOUR MARK.
GET SET.
DRAW!
HEY!
WOW!
WELL,
LOOKIT
THAT!

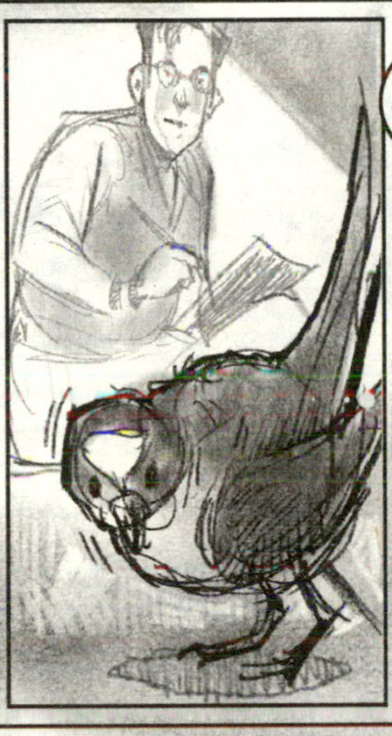

HEY--
YOU'RE DRAWING THE SAME THING I AM! THAT'S AGAINST THE RULES.

IT IS NOT. STOP GOOFING AROUND AND DRAW.

OH NO!
LOOK WHAT YOU DID, MAK!

WELL, IT DOESN'T MATTER BECAUSE I COULD DRAW THAT BIRD WITH MY EYES CLOSED!
NO DRAWING WITH EYES CLOSED. THAT'S AGAINST THE RULES TOO!
STOP BEING SILLY AND DRAW!

DONE YET?
SHUSH.

OKAY!
TIME'S UP!
LET'S COMPARE.

I DON'T KNOW.
MY DRAWING IS SO GOOD.
I DON'T WANT TO
EMBARRASS YOU.
C'MON, MAK.
PUT YOUR DRAWING
NEXT TO MINE.
OKAY.
BUT I WARNED
YOU.

Mari
MAK

HOW DO YOU DO THAT?
WHAT?

WHAT DO YOU MEAN, "WHAT?"?
THIS IS AMAZING! THE SWALLOW LOOKS
LIKE IT COULD FLY OFF THE PAPER!
WELL...

I GUESS
I JUST LET MY EYES
TELL MY BRAIN TO MAKE MY
HAND DRAW WHAT I'VE
BEEN LOOKING AT.

OH, C'MON!
IF IT WERE THAT SIMPLE,
EVERYONE COULD
DRAW.
I DUNNO.
DRAWING MAKES ME
FEEL GOOD.

YOU'RE SOMETHING SPECIAL, KIDDO.
BUT NOT ABNORMAL, RIGHT?!

RIGHT! SPECIAL! NOT ABNORMAL. NOW LET'S GO EAT. I'M STARVING.

YOU'RE ALWAYS STARVING.
THAT'S TRUE.

IT'S GONNA BE FUN TO WATCH YOU DO ALL THE LAUNDRY.
MAK. YOU KNOW I WON.

BUT DO I? THE JUDGES ARE UNDECIDED.
THEY ARE NOT!

I TELL YA WHAT--WE'LL CALL IT A DRAW.
NO!

GET IT? WE'LL CALL IT A DRAW!
MAK!
OH, ALL RIGHT. YOU WON.

1. THAT'LL TEACH THEM

It was a greyhound, my father said, a kind of dog, painted on the side of the bus. It didn't look like a dog. Not in the least. Trust me. If I were going to draw a dog, it wouldn't look like that thing. I was trying to figure out what this "dog" thing actually looked like when the bus pulled away, taking my brother off to the army. I waved to him. The windows were so dirty, I couldn't tell if he was waving back. So I waved harder. While I was waving, I noticed a suspicious-looking dust cloud rising up behind the bus. It loomed over my parents and me and took on the appearance of a hammer. I was sure it was up to no good. Luckily, a breeze grabbed ahold of it and tossed the dust hammer onto the side of the road.

I wish I hadn't been so concerned about the dust-cloud hammer, because by the time I'd confirmed that it wasn't going to clobber us, I realized that the bus was very, very far away. A moment later it and Mak were gone, disappearing behind a distant hill. I kept waving anyway.

If he'd been there, Mak would've laughed at me.

Hey, kabocha-head! I could hear him say. *Get a load of you worrying about a dust cloud. You and your crazy imagination!*

I rubbed my head where I imagined Mak would've applied his noogies. Funny thing was, I'd always hollered and squealed in the past when he rubbed my head with his knuckles. But now I actually missed them, Mak and his noogies. I pictured Mak's face, his eyes and eyebrows and the silly-looking glasses he wore, the way the little scar over his lip would tilt upward when he smiled. I jumped when Mama called my name.

"Come along, Mari," said Mama as she and Father started the long walk back to the barracks. (Like all the other grown-ups at the camp, they always spoke in Japanese. They had emigrated from Japan and didn't learn English when they were growing up, the way Mak and I did. We spoke in Japanese too when we talked with them, though when it was just Mak and me, we spoke English like the other kids. So as you read, just imagine our conversations are all in Japanese.)

"Mari!" said Father. "It's dinnertime! Come along."

Dinner? Honestly, Father! Mak is going to war on a dirty bus with a stupid dog thing painted on the side of it, and all you care about is dinner. I stood there for a moment, furious, thinking about dust clouds that looked like hammers, about my selfish big brother who'd made a stupid decision to go to war without discussing it with me first, and about my father needing to go eat another piece of boiled SPAM in the mess hall.

It was right then that I decided I wouldn't talk anymore.

I remember saying to myself, *I know what'll teach them. I'm not going to talk anymore.* Later on I added, *Or at least until Mak comes home.* But I didn't add that part till I'd spent a few days not talking. Take it from me, not talking is not easy.

"Mari! Please," hollered Father.

I spun about, stomped after my parents, and caught up to them. As we passed the guard post by the front gate, the sentry smiled at me. I stuck out my tongue.

That'll teach him, too.

HOW COULD YOU JOIN THE ARMY, MAKOTO? THEY ARE THE ONES WHO PUT US IN HERE!
IT'S THE RIGHT THING TO DO, FATHER. AND YOU KNOW IT.
DON'T YOU REMEMBER HOW IT WAS WHEN WE GOT HERE? THE RIOTS! MEN WERE SHOT BY THE SOLDIERS! PEOPLE WERE BEATEN FOR WORKING WITH THE ADMINISTRATION!
I WAS HERE. I SAW ALL OF IT. YOU'RE NOT GOING TO CHANGE MY MIND.

THEY WILL CALL YOU A TRAITOR!
I DON'T CARE WHAT PEOPLE CALL ME.
YOU MUST STOP THIS!
I MADE MY CHOICE, FATHER. I'M GONNA DO THIS.
WHY WON'T YOU LISTEN TO ME?
I COULD ASK YOU THE SAME QUESTION.

RESIGN! QUIT THE ARMY NOW BEFORE IT'S TOO LATE!
I'M IN. AND I'M GONNA DO MY PART.

THEN YOU ARE A FOOL!
I HAVE A FOOL FOR A SON!
ICHIRO!

A FOOL! THAT'S ALL I AM TO YOU, FATHER?!

I'M STILL HERE, FATHER.

ICHIRO.

PLEASE.
TALK TO YOUR SON.

WHY SHOULD I TALK IF HE WILL NOT LISTEN?

G'BYE, MOM. I'LL BE BACK LATER TO GET MY STUFF. WHEN HE'S NOT HERE.
THE BUS FOR BOOT CAMP LEAVES TOMORROW AFTERNOON FROM THE FRONT GATE.
GOODBYE, FATHER.

MAK!

2. TWO WEEKS IS A LONG, DUSTY TIME IN MANZANAR

Bad news: no mail from Mak! Not a single letter! I'd already written to him three times! And these weren't your average letters, either. These were four-page letters with long descriptions and drawings. I drew a picture of me and Mama and Father and the sentry by the front gate. And I drew the weird dog thing that was on the side of his bus and the dust cloud that turned into a hammer. The envelopes were stuffed and they needed extra postage to mail. Father made me pay for the extra stamps.

And still no mail from Mak. Do people forget how to write when they join the army? Maybe he didn't even get there. Maybe he jumped off of that dirty bus and joined the circus and he was too busy cleaning up after the elephants to write to me. Anyway, I couldn't believe he hadn't written to me yet.

And just so you know, being silent hadn't been easy. Not long after I'd made my vow, I started wishing I'd thought of some less difficult manner of teaching everyone a lesson. It was about then that I came up with a good reason for keeping silent: maybe by staying quiet I was somehow helping Mak come home safe. I know, it's kind of crazy and I'm not sure about the logic of that, but it felt like a better reason for keeping my vow than just to irritate Father.

For as long as I could remember, I was the one who'd done most of the talking in my family. Singing, too. And while Father was not a fan of my talking, he very much disliked my singing. He would put up with it, though, in that grumpy way he puts up with things he doesn't like. As far as my more recent decision not to talk was concerned, well, I was fairly certain he hated it. You'd think he would've appreciated my silence, seeing as he disliked my "jabbering" as much as he did. But not so. Mama, on the other hand, took my silence much better than Father. That was understandable. In the best of times, Father was a surly grump and Mama was, well, Mama. She could make sweet things out of sour.

I remember after Pearl Harbor when the FBI came and took our radio. Mama waited till they'd driven out of sight and then put a record on the phonograph, turned it up loud, and went right back to doing whatever she'd been doing before they arrived. Father? He stomped outside and slammed the front door, something he never did. And when we learned that the government was sending us to live in this dusty, frying-pan prison camp, Mama simply got busy: busy selling the farm and busy packing. Father? He fumed and snorted, staring at our fields and mumbling to himself about how little money we'd received for the farm and that we were being punished for a crime we didn't commit.

I remember waking one night to the sound of him smashing stuff in the kitchen. This scared me. But it didn't last. Father may come to a boil pretty quick, but he cools down even quicker.

Okay, back to my decision to stop talking; as I said, it was something that Father simply couldn't accept. Not only was it not acceptable, it was, to him, abnormal. And for Father, abnormal is the worst thing a person can be. One night during our walk home from the mess hall, Father knelt down and took my hands in his and looked me in the eye.

"Mari, this willful silence of yours must end. It is abnormal," he said.

"Ichiro, please," said Mama. "She's just upset over Mak leaving."

Father stood, frowning, his arms folded.

"Aki, we cannot simply ignore Mari's abnormal behavior."

Abnormal. There it was again. That word came out of Father's mouth like it tasted bad.

"She is becoming the object of scorn!"

Mama took my hand and started walking us back to our barracks.

"Mari is fine," Mama said over her shoulder. "Please relax, Ichiro. You're going to have a fit."

"I do not feel like I will have a fit," Father grumbled as he fell in behind us. (I made a mental note to myself: *Draw Father having a fit when we get home.*)

3. THE CLUCKING SISTERS

Still no mail came from Mak. What was wrong with him? How could he do this to me? He made me so angry! If he had been there right then, Mak would've been the person I wouldn't talk to the most! Ha! But honestly, three weeks was a long time to wait for a letter in a sweaty, nowhere place like Manzanar with nothing to do.

Well, that wasn't exactly true. There were things to do. Such as chores. There were always lots of those. Giving me chores to do was Father's way of paying me back for being abnormal. I hated chores. And doing laundry was the worst one of all. Oh, I just hated folding the laundry. Why fold it when you're only going to wear it again anyway?

But let's not dwell on laundry. On the bright side, I'd gotten pretty good at being silent. And I was quite proud of myself, because it hadn't been easy. A lot of grown-ups seemed to take my silence as a personal insult. They'd ask me a question and I'd just smile at them and wouldn't answer. Most grown-ups hate when kids do that kind of thing. But others thought my being silent was just a silly thing, something to laugh at and forget.

Being silent did, however, bring some pleasant surprises. For instance, I was happy to notice the irritation my silence caused our gossiping neighbors, the Chiba sisters. They lived next door to our barracks. Father called them the Clucking Sisters because they were always gossiping. They couldn't stand my silence. I couldn't stand their clucking. I spent many happy hours drawing the Chiba sisters. I really enjoyed turning them into chickens.

There was a big open space where everyone in our barracks hung their laundry. On Tuesday mornings it was my job to collect the dry clothes from the line. Many days the clothes were covered with dust, and I'd have to beat them with a stick to get the dust out before folding. Have I said how much I hate folding laundry? Anyway, I remember the Clucking Sisters watching me as I watched them. When I'd finished folding, I picked up my basket and walked past them, heading for home.

"Good morning, Mari," said Clucker #1.

"Hello, Mari," said Clucker #2.

I smiled at them and kept on walking.

"Mari," said Clucker #1. "It's rude not to say hello."

They didn't care about me saying hello. I'd walked past them dozens of times and they'd never even smiled at me. They just wanted to trick me into talking, that's all. Instead I did a little pirouette and walked on. I could hear them clucking behind me.

"Such a strange child," said Clucker #1.

"Cluck, cluck, cluck," said Clucker #2.

Inside our barracks, I began to fold our clothes. Father

stepped in. He was holding a small bundle of mail. MAIL!

"Mari, where is Mother?" said Father.

I dropped what I was folding and rushed over to make a grab at the mail. Father saw me coming and held everything above his head.

"Hey, stop it!" he cried.

Then he dropped it all on the floor.

"Look what you've done!" said Father. "I hope there was nothing breakable in this package."

I looked at the address. It was from Mak to me! Father picked the package up. I tried to grab it. He held it above his head. I danced around him, jumping and grabbing.

"Mari!" said Father. "Would you please stop it!"

I stopped jumping and stepped back. Father sat on his bed. I tried begging and gave him my best wide-eyed, suffering-child look.

"Stop this silliness, Mari! You're not the only one to get mail from your brother. You can open this when you have found your mother and brought her here."

I frowned.

"Hurry now, go," said Father, waving his hand in the direction of the door.

I knew exactly where Mama was. I raced out the door and through the camp, kicking up dust. I turned a corner and ran right into Mama. She was making her way back from taking a shower in the washing barracks.

"Oh! Mari!" cried Mama.

I grabbed her arm and started to pull.

"What's going on?" she said.

I gave her my best smile, waggled my eyebrows up and down, then nodded in the direction of our barracks.

"What do you want?" asked Mama.

I continued pulling and waggling my eyebrows.

"Oh, all right, Mari, I'm coming," laughed Mama.

We made our way into the space for drying laundry. The Chiba sisters were still there, folding and gossiping. I was walking backward, shuffling along as I pulled Mama. I wasn't looking and bumped into one of them.

"Oh, honestly!" said one Clucker.

"Have you ever . . . ?" said another.

"I'm sorry. Please excuse us," said Mama, bowing.

The Chiba sisters continued to cluck, something about the "rudeness of today's youth." Mama and I bowed one more time, and I took her arm and tugged her away from the Cluckers, all the way back to our barracks. Inside we found that Father had arrayed our mail on the small table.

"Oh, Aki, I'm sorry," he said. "Did she stop you from taking your shower?"

"No, no, I was finished," she replied. "Is there mail from Mak?!"

"Yes," said Father.

I grabbed the package addressed to me, flopped to the floor by my bed, and tore into it. Inside I found beautiful, wonderful things. There was a letter from Mak and a knitted army cap! I quickly put the cap on my head. It was much too big, but to me it was a perfect fit. This was obviously the best hat ever made. How could it not be a perfect fit?

I unfolded the letter, but for some reason I just couldn't

read it. This was odd because I'm a good reader. I stared at the marks Mak had made on the paper and couldn't figure them out. I told myself, *Stop being silly and read Mak's letter!* But I just couldn't. I was startled when drops of water slid off my face and onto the paper, further blurring the words.

"Mari, what's wrong?" asked Mama. "Has Mak written something sad?"

I looked at Mama, held up the letter, and wobbled the pages, hoping she'd understand that to mean, *For some reason I've forgotten how to read.* She sat herself on the floor beside me.

"Oh, my dear," she said. "Here, let's read it together, shall we?"

Mama pulled a hanky from her pocket, sat beside me, and wiped the tears from my face. I rested my head on her shoulder and she read Mak's letter out loud.

June 20, 1944
Camp Shelby
Mississippi
Hey, kiddo,

How goes life? How are Mom and Pop? I hope you are all well and happy. I am doing just fine. And I'm sorry I haven't written sooner. But this is the first time I've been able to sit down with a pen and paper.

It took us quite a while to get from Manzanar to Camp Shelby in Mississippi. We zigzagged back and forth, picking up other recruits along the way. I hope I never have to sleep on a bus ever again!

Man, what a long bus ride.

Once we arrived at boot camp, there was no end to the excitement! Our drill sergeants met us at the bus—not a bad bunch of fellows.
WELCOME TO CAMP SHELBY.

GEEZ, IT'S REALLY HOT!
GOLLY! YOU FELLAS MUST BE PLUMB WORE OUT AFTER THAT LONG BUS RIDE. HOW'S YOUR BACK?
ACTUALLY, MY BACK IS KINDA SORE. THANKS FOR ASKING.
WELL, I DON'T GIVE A RAT'S FUZZY BUTT ABOUT HOW SORE YOU ARE!
GET OFF THAT BUS!
SHUT UP!
AND LINE UP!
WELL, LOOKIT THIS!
HOW'D A LITTLE TURD LIKE YOU GIT INTO MY ARMY!
YOU TAKE THAT UGLY FACE OF YOURS OVER THERE AND TOE THAT LINE. MOVE IT, BOY!

TOE THAT LINE!
OKAY! GEEZ!
EYES STRAIGHT AHEAD, HALF-PINT!
MOVE IT! MOVE IT! MOVE IT!
ALL RIGHT, LISTEN UP! I AM SERGEANT DEVERS. IT IS MY JOB TO TURN YOU SORRY SLOBS INTO SOLDIERS. YOU WILL ADDRESS ME AS SERGEANT, NOT SIR. IS THAT CLEAR? SOUND OFF!
WILL DO, SIR.
YUP.
GOTCHA, SIR!
YOU BET, SARGE.

DID I NOT JUST TELL YOU TO NOT CALL ME SIR?!
WELL?!
I...
UH...
WHAT A BUNCH OF PEA BRAINS. THEY JUST KEEP GETTIN' DUMBER AND DUMBER.
YOU SAID IT.
ALRIGHT, TAKE 'EM OVER AND GET THEIR HEADS SHAVED.
WILL DO, SERGEANT.
EYES FRONT!
TIME FOR A LITTLE TRIM OFF THE TOP, BOYS! LEFT FACE. FORWARD, MARCH!
HANDS OUTTA POCKETS, KNUCKLEHEAD!
YES, SERGEANT!
BARBER

NOT LOOKING FORWARD TO THIS.
ME NEITHER.
HOLD STILL.
RUBBING IT AIN'T GONNA MAKE IT GROW BACK ANY FASTER! GIT OUT THERE AND TOE THAT LINE!
YES, SERGEANT!
YOU HEARD THE SERGEANT! MOVE IT, NUMBSKULL!

EQUIPMENT
I look pretty good with short hair, if I do say so myself. Right after we got our hair cut, they sent us over to the equipment depot to get our gear. Now I have everything I need to at least look like a soldier.
I DO HOPE I'M NOT BEING TOO ROUGH ON YOU BOYS. HOW 'BOUT Y'ALL TROT OVER TO YOUR BARRACKS, PUT ON THEM NICE, NEW FATIGUES, AND MEET ME BACK HERE? SOUND GOOD?
YES, SERGEANT!
MOVE IT!
OOPS!
Y'SEE, I'D REALLY LIKE FOR US TO BE FRIENDS.
BUT...

...YOU BOYS
JUST KEEP ON DISAPPOINTIN'
ME.

MY GOODNESS.
SO SLOW.
WHY, IT'S
ALMOST AS IF Y'ALL ARE TRYIN'
TO TICK ME OFF.

BOYS, IT'S MY JOB TO TURN Y'ALL INTO A FIERCE FIGHTING UNIT.
Y'ALL WANNA BE A FIERCE FIGHTING UNIT.
WELL, DONCHA?!
YES, SERGEANT!
YES, SERGEANT!
YES, SERGEANT!
GOOD. VERY GOOD.
CORPORAL, LET'S GIVE THESE BOYS A LITTLE TOUR OF THE CAMP BEFORE BED.
OKAY?
SURE THING, SARGE.
AND BE GENTLE WITH THESE BOYS. IT'S THEIR FIRST DAY. WE DON'T WANT TO TIRE THEM OUT.
HEH, HEH.

CARRY ON, CORPORAL.
WILL DO, SARGE.
LISTEN UP. I'M CORPORAL SCHMIDT. THE SERGEANT WANTS ME TO LEAD YOU ON SOME LIGHT EXERCISE.
I THINK A LITTLE FIVE-MILE HIKE SHOULD DO THE TRICK.
FOLLOW MY CADENCE! FORWARD-MARCH!
LEFT, LEFT, LEFT, RIGHT, LEFT! YOU HAD A GOOD JOB BUT YOU LEFT! YOU LEFT, RIGHT, LEFT!

KEEP MOVING! DO NOT STOP!
I CAN'T SWIM!
SNAKES?!
THIS IS MORE THAN FIVE MILES.
SILENCE IN THE RANKS!
OH MAN, I'M GONNA VOMIT!
WE PASSED FIVE MILES ABOUT FIVE MILES AGO.
I'M GONNA VOMIT!
STOP SAYING "VOMIT." YOU'RE GONNA MAKE ME THROW UP!
KEEP IT UP AND YOU'RE GONNA FIND THE BUSINESS END OF MY BOOT ON YOUR BUTT!

HEADS UP! SHOULDERS BACK! OU WILL MARCH THROUGH THAT GATE WITH PRIDE!
CAMP SHELBY
COMPANY-- HALT!
HMMM...
YOU ARE LATE, CORPORAL.

THIS IS VERY DISAPPOINTING. WHAT IS THE REASON FOR YOUR TARDINESS?
SORRY, SERGEANT. NO EXCUSE.

DON'T APOLOGIZE, CORPORAL. IT'S NOT YOUR FAULT. IT'S THESE RECRUITS!

THEY'RE THE WORST RECRUITS I'VE EVER SEEN! A BUNCH OF SLOW, STUPID, SLOVENLY NUMBSKULLS! A DISGRACE TO THE ARMY!

THEY'RE HOPELESS. I JUST DON'T KNOW WHAT TO DO WITH THEM.
WE COULD SHIP 'EM OVER TO THE NAVY.
THEY AIN'T TOO PICKY.
NO, THAT WOULDN'T BE FAIR TO THE NAVY, CORPORAL.
OR TO THE MARINES.
THE MARINES?
WAIT! I HAVE IT! I WON'T SHIP THEM OUT! INSTEAD I'LL DEDICATE EVERY WAKING MOMENT TO MOLDING THESE BUMS INTO THE FINEST COMPANY IN THE ARMY!
ARE YOU SURE ABOUT THIS, SERGEANT?
WITH ALL MY HEART, CORPORAL.
IN THE MEANTIME, LET'S GET THESE NITWITS OFF TO BED. YOU MAY PROCEED, CORPORAL.
WILL DO, SERGEANT.
COMPANY! FRONT RANK-- RIGHT FACE! FORWARD, MARCH!
ENTER THE BARRACKS. LIGHTS OUT IN FIVE!

WELL, LOOKIT THIS! ALL READY FOR BED. HOW NICE. DID EVERYONE HAVE FUN ON THEIR FIRST DAY OF BOOT CAMP?
YES, SERGEANT!
GOOD!
BECAUSE THAT'S THE LAST FUN YOU'RE GONNA HAVE FOR THE NEXT SIX WEEKS!
ESPECIALLY YOU, FOUR EYES!
WHAT'S WITH THEM GOOFY SPECS?
YOU TRYIN' TO LOOK LIKE MR. TŌJŌ, THE EMPEROR OF JAPAN? SPEAK UP, BOY!
UH... N-NO, SERGEANT!

I GOT MY EYE ON YOU, MR. TŌJŌ. AIN'T GONNA BE NO EMPEROR OF JAPAN IN MY ARMY.
YOU HEAR ME?
YES, SERGEANT!
AND I GOT MY EYE ON THE REST OF YOU BUMS TOO!
I'LL MAKE SOLDIERS OUT OF Y'ALL IF IT KILLS YOU!
IS THAT CLEAR?!
YES, SERGEANT!
GOOD. HIT THE SACK.
LIGHTS OUT!

Our drill sergeant is an okay guy. He likes to give us a pep talk before lights-out each night. That's about all there is to say here. I hope you like your hat. It's probably too hot to wear it right now, but I thought you'd like it anyway. Be good for Mom and Pop.

Love, your brother Mak

Mama and I sat quietly for a minute. I thought about Mak and his letter. There was something about what Mak was saying, or maybe about what he wasn't saying, that seemed strange to me. Everything sounded so happy, as if his joining the army had all been just a sunny, fun day at the lake. It didn't sound real. And it just didn't sound like the Mak I knew.

I looked around and saw that Father was gone. I hadn't noticed him leave. My eye caught the framed photo of Mak that sat on Mama's bureau. He wore that crooked smile of his in this photo, and he seemed to be saying, *That's right, kiddo. Can't put anything over on you. Things ain't what they appear in this here army.*

Mama used her hanky again to wipe my eyes and then her own.

"I see that Mak has sent you a nice hat," Mama sighed. "He is a good brother."

I grabbed the sides of the hat and pulled it down over my eyes. Mama hugged me.

"And you are a silly girl."

4. DUST. FOOD. MORE DUST.

Don't get me started on the food. Okay, I have to say at least one thing about it. When we first arrived at Manzanar, the food was horrible. No, it was worse than horrible. How do I help you understand just how horrible? Hmmm . . . let me see, oh, I know—this is one of the things they gave us to eat the first week we arrived. (You better be sitting down, because this is gonna make you feel sick.) Here we go—canned peaches over cold rice. That's right. Peaches and rice! For dinner! They also dumped these little meat things they called Vienna sausages on top of that disgusting pile of mush. These Vienna sausages weren't the wonderful sort of sausage you might eat with eggs and toast for breakfast. They were these little meat blobs, mushy and tasteless. It's true that, as time went on, the food got better. It helped that Issei and Nisei (first- and second-generation Japanese Americans) with cooking experience took over the job of making the food. But c'mon, peaches and sausages on cold rice!

Horrible, right?!

This particular day Mama and I rose early and made our

way to the mess hall. I brought my drawing pad with me. Mama had ordered me some drawing pencils from Sears Roebuck. They had been shipped to the camp, and Father had brought them home from the mail room the night before. I couldn't wait to try them out. The wind was quiet that morning for a change, and so we arrived at the mess hall without the usual coating of dust.

Dust. From our first day at Manzanar, we battled with the dust and the windstorms and we always lost. It didn't matter whether we were inside or out. The dust was so fine that it found its way into everything. Our clothes, our mouths, our food, our eyes. Everything.

We found Oba-chan Yuki waiting at the door to the hall all alone. She was one of the oldest people in the camp. "Oba-chan" means "auntie," but she wasn't really my aunt. We called all the older ladies Oba-chan. I liked that. And I liked Oba-chan Yuki not just because she was nice to me, but because she was a really good storyteller. Sometimes she would give us a quick story after breakfast. I liked to draw while she talked. I was glad I'd brought my sketchbook.

"Good morning, Oba-chan Yuki," said Mama, bowing.

"Good morning," she replied, bowing in return.

The door opened. We shuffled inside with Oba-chan, got our breakfast, and made our way to a table. I was, of course, wearing my new cap. While I still felt it to be the finest cap in the world, I'd noticed that it had a definite downside—it itched. Not just a little itchy, but fiercely itchy. That didn't matter, though. The hat could itch me until all the skin on my head fell off, and I'd still wear it.

The upside was that no other kid in the camp but me had an army cap, and I felt certain that I was the center of attention in the mess hall that morning. The Clucking Sisters had certainly gotten a good look at me. They were clucking up a storm over at their table, and when I stuck my tongue out at them, their clucking got a lot louder.

As usual, our table had a thin layer of dust on it. Mama and I wiped off a place for Oba-chan Yuki and ourselves. We sat, said a prayer, and began to eat. I'd noticed that elders like Oba-chan Yuki rarely talked while they ate. That morning was no different. I started drawing a picture of Oba-chan while I waited for her to finish eating. When she'd finished her breakfast—which appeared to be mostly thin slabs of fried SPAM washed down by hot tea—Oba-chan Yuki tapped me on my hand.

"I like your army hat," she said. "Where did you get it?"

I started to feel a little shy. I looked at Mama for help. She just smiled. So I crossed my arms on the table and hid my face.

"What's wrong? Is she sleepy?" said Oba-chan Yuki.

Mama gently put her hand on Oba-chan Yuki's arm. "Her brother gave her the hat, Oba-chan. And Mari has given up talking until her brother returns from the army."

I looked up. Oba-chan Yuki was staring at me with her little black eyes.

"Ah," said Oba-chan. "A vow of silence. Is that so?"

She took a sip of her tea, then ran a crooked finger over her chin.

"You know," said Oba-chan, "you remind me of the

suzume in that fairy tale. You know that story about the sparrow?"

I sat up, shook my head no.

"Would you like to hear that story?"

I nodded yes! I pulled out my sketchbook and pencils.

"Good," said Oba-chan Yuki. "I will tell it to you. It's a good one. It starts out like this: Once upon a time there was a farmer and his wife. They lived up in the mountains." She pointed out the window toward the Sierra Nevada. The sun was up and the mountains were lit up like they were on fire.

"The farmer," Oba-chan Yuki continued, "he was such a nice man. Very kind. Always smiling. Whistled a lot too. On the other hand, his wife, well, she was a big complainer. Grumpy and sour. Always yapping. You know the type."

The three of us looked over at the table where the Clucking Sisters and their friends sat, sipping coffee and gossiping.

"As I was saying—gabby, grumpy, and sour. Spiteful, too," said Oba-chan Yuki. "And even though she had a nice husband, the wife was never satisfied. What's worse, she couldn't stand his pet sparrow. The farmer had saved the sparrow from a hawk and nursed her back to health. His wife just hated that. She didn't like how much time he spent teaching the sparrow to sing and do tricks, such as hang upside down on the clothesline or stand on her beak. A delightful bird, by the way. Beautiful singing, sweet and kind. Bashful, too. She would hide her face under her wing when the farmer praised her singing.

"But the wife, well, she just hated the whole thing. And one morning when the farmer headed out into the fields to begin the harvest, the wife prepared a bowl of starch to do the wash. She set the bowl outside for the sun to melt the starch, but the sparrow got to it before the sun did and gobbled it down. The wife found the sparrow preening herself after the splendid meal. This infuriated the nasty woman, and she decided to do the meanest thing. She grabbed a pair of scissors and cut out the sparrow's little tongue. The sparrow quickly flew away. When the farmer got home, he called for the sparrow but, of course, got no answer. The wife told him a lie. The sparrow had grown tired of him, she said, and left him for a better master.

"Now, who knows why, but the farmer loved his wife. Yet in spite of this love, he knew full well that she was capable of pettiness and lying. So that night he went looking for his little sparrow friend. And don't you know, it took him forever but he finally found the sparrow's home. It was in an enormous tree. And there must've been thousands of sparrows flying all about. He knocked on the tree, and they invited him to climb up and have a cup of tea. Right away he apologized for his wife's terrible behavior. The sparrow told him not to worry. It turned out that his little sparrow was magical! There was no way that a mortal could harm her. Her tongue was healed, and she was so happy to see the farmer! She called all the sparrows together and announced that there would be a party! They had a grand old time. Lots of singing and dancing. And such food!

"Eventually the farmer grew tired and said that he'd have to start home soon—his crops wouldn't be able to tend themselves and so forth. The sparrow was so touched by the kindness of her friend. She ordered her flock to bring two wicker baskets for his homeward gift. One basket was very heavy and one very light. The farmer was told that he could choose one of the two to take home. He thanked his friends for the gift, looked at the two baskets, and, thinking that he wouldn't want to take more than his share, told them that he would take the lighter of the two. The sparrows bid their friend a fond farewell and sang delightful songs for him as he began his journey homeward.

"You can imagine the sort of unpleasant welcome he got when he arrived home. 'Where have you been?' howled his wife. But, boy oh boy, was she ever happy when she saw what poured out of the lighter basket—there was gold and silver, and jade and jewels, and silk and coral and much more. All in that little basket! However, her feelings changed again when he revealed that he'd taken the lighter of the two baskets. She called him a fool, a dolt, a dummy. How could he have chosen the smaller basket of treasure? She put on her shawl and told the farmer to make dinner while she was gone.

"Off she marched, taking the straightest road to the sparrow's house. The sparrows weren't too happy to see the nasty old wife, but as she had traveled so far, they couldn't deny her a cup of tea and a bite to eat before sending her along. After she'd gobbled down the tea and treats, the wife stood up and rudely said, 'I can't waste any more time here, so you might as well bring out the baskets.' And that's exactly what those sparrows did—they brought out the heavy basket and another light basket.

"Now, of course, the greedy wife grabbed the bigger basket, and without even a quick 'So long,' she scurried out the door and headed for home. But a mile or two from the farm, she decided to empty her basket on the ground to get a good look at her treasure. 'Who knows,' she said to herself, 'maybe I'll buy my own farm with this fortune and say good-bye to my good-for-nothing husband.' But when she turned the basket over, she found it was filled not with gems and gold and jewels, but with lots and lots of tiny gremlins and ugly imps and unsavory demons. They began to poke her, and pinch her, pull her hair and torment her. This was too much! She ran down the road, not toward home, but away from the farm and her husband! On and on she ran, howling and crying, with those little demons tormenting her all the while. And you know, they say that to this day you can hear her up in those mountains, yowling and shrieking as she runs up and down, up and down!

"The end!" Oba-chan Yuki laughed. "Good story, neh?"

Mama and I clapped. Oba-chan Yuki smiled at me. I smiled back.

"Mari," she said. "Would you mind if I look at your drawings?"

I handed her my sketchbook.

"This is lovely, Mari," said Oba-chan Yuki, holding up my sketchbook. "Very fine." She turned to Mama. "Do you know my daughter, Eunice? Eunice the watercolor painter? I've told you about her, yes?"

"Oh, yes," said Mama. "We saw some of her paintings at the art show last month. Just wonderful! Did she really make artwork for the *Reader's Digest* magazine before the war?"

"Yes, she has had success with her artwork," said Oba-chan Yuki proudly. "I tell you what—what would you say to introducing your Mari to my Eunice?"

"Oh, I like that idea," said Mama. "Don't you, Mari?"

I had been staring at the drawing I'd done of the sparrow and glanced up to see Oba-chan Yuki and Mama smiling at me. I could see that the Clucking Sisters were staring at me too. There were just too many grown-ups looking at me. I nodded quickly, then pulled my hat down over my eyes and hid.

"Heh, heh!" chuckled Oba-chan Yuki. "She is bashful just like the suzume." Leaning on her cane, she began to rise. "Well, time for my morning nap."

Mama offered to walk her home, but Oba-chan Yuki said no, she would be fine on her own. Mama said goodbye, we bowed, and Oba-chan began to shuffle toward the door, then stopped and turned back.

"Yes," said Oba-chan Yuki, looking at me. "I think you and my Eunice will get along nicely."

5. CAMOUFLAGE

This is what I have to say about school in the camp: I went to school. It wasn't fun. The end.

I'm not trying to be funny. I'm just being honest. I didn't like school in the camp and I don't have much to say about it. Okay, I'll say a few things about it:

I'd liked school just fine back at home. I'd liked all the subjects, and I'd had lots of friends, too. But for some reason I just couldn't find something or somebody to like at the camp school.

When we first got to the camp, not all the buildings were finished, so the teachers would sit outside with us in the shade and teach us to read and write and do math. That wasn't too bad. Eventually they got around to finishing the "school." The insides looked like average classrooms, I guess. Except there were no chairs at first. That's right, you heard me—no chairs! We had to sit on old pieces of newspaper on the floor. And sometimes we'd run out of simple stuff, like paper and chalk. That had certainly never happened back at my school at home. And of course, my school at home wasn't surrounded by a barbed-wire fence.

I was wrong in saying I didn't have any friends, though. At first I would play with Marion and sometimes Ruth. But mostly I spent my extra time at school drawing and reading. I'm pretty smart, and I would finish my classwork quickly. Then, instead of going outside to play with the other kids, I would grab my sketchbook and draw. Sometimes I'd sit in the shade outside and read. I did a lot of drawing and reading.

For some reason it annoyed the kids that I liked to read and draw as much as I did. I got teased a lot. Especially by the boys. Every now and then I'd find that someone had taken my sketchbook and torn out one of my sketches. This was very upsetting to me. But the teacher never did anything about it. She thought my drawing was a bit of a nuisance anyway. "You shouldn't be scribbling all the time, Mari," she'd say. I found my best revenge was to draw a picture of whichever boy had stolen my artwork. I'd draw it so everyone could see. Then I'd draw him in some diapers, crying like a baby. Some boys would get very angry at this. But they never stole my artwork again.

As far as my decision to stop talking was concerned, well, that got an even worse reception. Everyone seemed to take my silence personally. It was a popular game to see who'd be the first to get me to say something like "Stop it!" because my hair had been yanked for the hundredth time. So I kept to myself. And like I said, I'd draw and read.

There was, however, one part of school at camp that I did like very much. That part was lunch with Mama. Sometimes she would meet me outside and we'd sit on a shaded bench by the former camouflage factory and eat sandwiches she'd made. Mama used to work in the factory before it shut down. After that, she worked at the farm, picking cabbage.

The cavernous building had been taken over by swarms of little birds. Father said they were cliff swallows. There were unfinished sheets of camouflage hanging from the rafters of the abandoned factory. I loved to watch the swallows zip in and out of the camouflage as it swayed in the wind.

Today Mama had packed SPAM and cabbage sandwiches with mustard. I'd never eaten SPAM till we came here. If we ever leave, I will never eat SPAM again.

Or cabbage. Or mustard.

"So, I saw you had another letter from Mak," said Mama after we'd eaten. "May I read it?" I nodded and pulled the letter from my jacket. Mama began to read out loud.

July 7, 1944
Camp Shelby
Dear Mari,

How are things in dusty old Manzanar? And Mom and Pop, how are they? I hope you are being good for them. For instance, you could do your chores with a smile every once in a while. Ha! I know that'll never happen. Especially when it's your turn to fold the laundry.

Anyway, thank you for the drawings you sent me. I've pinned them up behind my bunk. They're a big hit!

I thought I'd give you an idea of what a day in the army is like. So here is my boot camp schedule:

5 a.m.—Wake up!

5:30 a.m.—Chow time!

After breakfast we do chores. That's right! Even in the army we do chores! But here we call it cleanup duty. Mostly picking up trash and pushing piles of dirt from here to there. I've made a good friend already. His name is Whitey. He comes from Hawaii, an island called Kauai. He's taught me some Hawaiian words while we clean up the joint.

WHAT'S GOING ON HERE?
CLEANUP DUTY, SERGEANT.

YOU AND THE EMPEROR OF JAPAN ARE SPYIN' ON THE US ARMY. AIN'T YA?!
NO, SERGEANT!

YOU THINK YOU'RE AN AMERICAN, DONCHA?
RED-BLOODED! JUST LIKE YOU, SERGEANT!
YOU AIN'T LIKE ME, BOY.
AND YOU NEVER WILL BE.

NOW GIT BACK TO WORK!
YES, SERGEANT!

ROTTEN HAOLE!
WHAT'S A HAOLE?
A HAOLE IS A PUNK WHO THINKS HE'S BETTER THAN YOU JUST 'CAUSE HIS SKIN IS PINK...

...AND YOURS AIN'T.

10 a.m.—After cleanup duty we practice hand-to-hand fighting. Not my favorite.

1 p.m.—After lunch we do more drills. And more drills.

Noon—Just lik
home, I'm usu
pretty hungry
the time lunc
around. The
is even wors
Manzanar.
beans and
And SPA
If I neve
piece of
so happ

5 p.m.—By suppertime I'm usually so hungry that I'll eat anything they put on my plate. And I mean anything!

7 p.m.—Some nights after chow, they show us a movie!

8 p.m.—Last night we went for a swim after the movie.

9 p.m.—We're usually back in our bunks right after night exercise. Fellas goof around—play cards, read, and generally let off steam.

LIGHTS OUT, CHILDREN. SHUT YOUR YAPS AND HIT THE SACK!

I WILL SEE Y'ALL AT FIVE A.M. FOR ANOTHER GLORIOUS DAY IN THE ARMY.

10 p.m.—I don't think there's been a single night since I got here where, when my head hits that pillow, I haven't fallen fast asleep. Out like a light!

But things aren't too bad here. Certainly no worse than Manzanar. I hope you're taking good care of Mom and Pop. Mom wrote me about your refusing to talk till I come home. Thank you for thinking about me. But I hope you don't drive Mom and Pop crazy with any more protests on my behalf. Okay? And do me another favor—ask Pop to drop me a line. I know he's still sore at me, but I'd really like to hear from him.

Be good and be happy, your brother Mak

"Well," said Mama. "Your brother writes a lovely letter, don't you think?"

I nodded and leaned my head against her shoulder. We watched the swallows dart in and out of the factory, swooping about the fluttering camouflage. Some kids were frightened of the old building and thought it was haunted. They wouldn't walk anywhere near it, not in daylight and certainly not at night. Even though it had its spooky qualities, I liked it. During the day it looked like an old sailing ship to me. I imagined it coasting across the dusty floor of the camp when nobody was looking. But at night, when the wind howled and shook the old wooden ribs of the place and the camouflage flapped about, it was a scary sight to see. Just thinking about it gave me the chills. Even so, I still liked it.

"It's not right that your father hasn't written to Mak," Mama said, hugging me. "I'll speak to him about that."

She stood and pulled me up beside her. "Come along, my little suzume. Back to school for you and work for me."

That evening Mama, Father, and I ate dinner together in the mess hall. Since Mak had left and the beginning of my silent treatment, things could get testy at dinner.

"Mari, please, eat something," said Father. "You must eat."

He was just itching to use his favorite word on me. I could feel it. I rested my chin on my folded arms and stared at my tray, waiting. *Here it comes,* I thought.

"Aki, this is . . . well, this is abnormal," blurted Father. "She must eat."

Abnormal. There it was. Again.

"She will eat," said Mama. "Isn't that right, Mari?"

I just smiled and made a goofy face at the pile of steamed root vegetables on my plate. Mama laughed.

"Aki, this is not a joke," cried Father.

This caught the attention of the Clucking Sisters and their friends. They peered over their shoulders at us and made little clucking noises.

"Ichiro," murmured Mama.

"I'm sorry," Father whispered, "but children must eat. And that hat! She hasn't taken it off in weeks. It's starting to smell."

Mama picked up a cookie and wrapped it in a napkin. She put her hand on my shoulder and stood.

"We should go," she said. "It's time to visit the Children's Village."

Father and I followed Mama outside.

"Sometimes I feel that I am not listened to in this family," said Father.

"We listen to you," said Mama. "Don't we, Mari?"

I moved in between Mama and Father, hugging them both. Father showed a small smile.

As we made our way across the camp, the sun was setting behind the Sierra mountains. The day's heat flowed up from the dirt under our feet. Soon we came under the mountain's shadow and it quickly grew chilly. That's the way it was in Manzanar—while the sun was up, it was hot as a griddle, but when it went down, it would get very cold, very fast.

The Children's Village was the place where the soldiers had put all the orphan children back in '42. Mama and Father had us begin helping out at the orphanage soon after it opened. I suppose they did this to keep us busy and not fuming over being stuck in a prison in a desert. For me, I just went for the babies. Babies made me happy.

We walked into the center of the three barracks that held the Village. Father opened the door, and we found the hall filled with the happy noise of children playing. Some of the older children were helping the staff clear away the remains of dinner. Father began to help put away chairs and tables. Mama and I entered an adjoining room, the nursery. Inside were seven cribs, each holding a baby. A nurse was changing the diaper of one of the children. Mama offered to help with another.

I made my way over to Keiko's crib. Keiko and I were best friends. She saw me and began to squeal and coo. I picked her up, and she grabbed my hair and my hat. I swooped her about the room. We laughed together. Oh, and just so you know, I'd decided that laughing wasn't part of my silence. I used to tell stories and sing lullabies to the babies. Keiko seemed to miss my songs. I did my best to make up for my silence by laughing with her a lot.

Some nights I would sit side by side with Keiko and we'd draw pictures. The baby crayons were thick and the paper was rough. She loved to rub the red crayons back and forth across the sheet of paper. Sometimes she'd rub so hard, she'd tear the paper, and this would make her cry. She also seemed to love the flavor of the crayons. I took a small bite once and it tasted awful. But Keiko loved to chew on them, and I'd have to pull the crayons from her mouth when she'd start to swallow the little bits that she'd managed to chew off with her tiny teeth.

That night I brought Keiko from one crib to the next, letting her have a quick baby conversation with the other children. Eventually the nurse handed me Keiko's bottle. I carefully followed the procedure I'd been shown, first sitting in a rocking chair, then testing the milk's warmth and placing a small towel on my shoulder, and lastly nestling Keiko in my arms and letting her drink to her fill. When the meal was finished, I would burp my sleepy Keiko, place her back into her crib, and carefully wrap her in her blanket. I looked up to see Father and Mama watching me. Time to go home.

We made our farewells to the staff, buttoned our jackets, and stepped out into the chilly darkness. Mama took the cookie she had wrapped in the napkin and fed pieces of it to me like a mama bird feeds her chick. I flapped my elbows like they were little sparrow wings.

"My little suzume!" Mama said, and laughed.

Father sighed.

I flapped my suzume wings all the way home.

5A. I LOST MY SKETCHBOOK!

All of my best drawings were in that sketchbook! I was sure one of the Clucking Sisters took it. Or maybe one of the boys in my class. This is terrible!

5B. OKAY, I FOUND IT

It was in the bottom of the clothes basket underneath all the folded laundry. Another reason to never do the laundry. Sorry if I got you all worked up about me losing my sketchbook. Sometimes I can be a little excitable.

But not abnormal.

July 23, 1944
Camp Shelby
Dear Mari,

How're things, kabocha-head? I miss giving you noogies on your noggin. I'd appreciate it if you'd apply some to your head from time to time. Just be careful of bruising your brain. Ha!

Mom tells me you are taking good care of the babies in the orphanage and that you've made friends with one. That's great! Let me tell you about one of the friends I've made in boot camp. His name is Kazuo—Kaz for short. He's from Hawaii. Speaking of short, he's probably the shortest man in camp. But he's about as wide as he is tall. And he can be a bit short tempered.

I HATE SPAM. WHAT'S THE BIG DEAL?
YOU BETTAH WATCH THAT TALK, BOY!
HOLD ON. YOU ACTUALLY LIKE SPAM?
DAS RIGHT, MAINLAND BOY.
I COULD EAT SPAM ALL DAY AND NIGHT AND NOT GET ENOUGH.
SO SHUT UP WITH TRASH-TALKIN' SPAM, OR YOU AND ME ARE GONNA SQUARE OFF.
GOT IT?
I AM NOT GOING TO FIGHT WITH YOU OVER LOUSY SPAM.
KEEP IT UP AND I'MA BUST YOU RIGHT IN THE CHOPS.
HEY, EASE UP, KAZ.
DIS AIN'T YOUR BEEF, WHITEY.
MAYBE. MAYBE NOT.
BUT NO NEED TO FLIP OUR LIDS WHILE THE CHOW IS HOT. LET'S RELAX AND EAT. SQUARE OFF LATER.
HUH?
HMMM...
GOOD THINKIN'.
BUT TELL YOUR KOTONK PAL TO KEEP HIS YAP SHUT ABOUT SPAM.
WILL DO.
MAK, DON'T SAY NO MORE ABOUT SPAM.
UH, SURE.

HEY, WHITEY, WHAT'S A KOTONK?
OH, THAT'S JUST A LITTLE JOKE WE HAWAIIAN BUDDHAHEADS HAVE ABOUT YOU MAINLAND BOYS.
OH YEAH? WHAT KINDA JOKE?

WELL, WE CALL YOU KOTONKS 'CAUSE THAT'S THE NOISE YOUR HEAD MAKES WHEN IT HITS THE FLOOR AFTER WE KNOCK YOU DOWN IN A FIGHT. KINDA LIKE A COCONUT WHEN IT HITS THE GROUND.
KOTONK! GET IT? IT'S FUNNY, RIGHT?
YOU'RE KIDDING. THAT'S NOT FUNNY.

IT'S A LITTLE FUNNY.
RIGHT, KAZ?
KOTONK! JUST LIKE A COCONUT. VERY FUNNY.

Kaz and I didn't get along at first. But things got better over time.

THINK IT'LL HELP?
NAH.
BUT AT LEAST WE CATCH A BREAK FROM ALL THOSE NOISY BUDDHAHEADS!
THE NEXT DAY...
HEY, HOW'S IT, MAINLAND BOY?
WHAT DO YOU WANT, KAZ?
ANSWER ME SOMETHING-- THEM HAOLE STICK YOU IN ONE OF THOSE CAMPS?
YES. ME AND MY FAMILY. WHAT ABOUT IT?
FAMILY?
YOU MEAN LIKE BABIES AND SUCH?
NO. NO BABIES IN MY FAMILY. JUST ME AND MY LITTLE SISTER AND MY PARENTS.
BUT THERE ARE LOTS OF FAMILIES WITH BABIES IN THE CAMP. LOTS OF OLD FOLKS, TOO. AND SICK PEOPLE. AND ORPHANS. THEY TOOK KIDS FROM ORPHANAGES AND STUCK THEM IN THE CAMP.

I'm glad you're making friends, Mari. It's good to have friends. I wish you, Mom, and Pop good health and happiness, always.

Love, your big brother Mak

6. OBA-CHAN YUKI'S CAVE

One morning as Mama and I were walking to breakfast, I began to think about Mak and how much I missed him. I had sent him a drawing I did of the sparrow. I was thinking about that drawing and wondering if it had arrived yet when we met Oba-chan Yuki on the way to the mess hall. She was moving slower than her normal slowness. Mama asked if she was okay. Oba-chan Yuki stopped and coughed. She reached out a hand and Mama steadied her.

"I am fine. The air is a little thick today, that's all."

I looked at Mama. Thick air? The air wasn't thick. There was hardly any dust in the air today. Oba-chan Yuki began to cough. It was one of those coughs that seem to never end. She began to wobble a bit. Mama took her arm.

"Please, Oba-chan," said Mama, worry plain on her face, "please come back to the barracks with us. You should lie down."

"Nah, nah," said Oba-chan Yuki. "I will be fine after I eat something."

Oba-chan Yuki coughed again. It was a chunky cough

and it went on for too long. She began to stumble, then fell to her knees.

"Oh, oh, let me help you!" exclaimed Mama. She put one hand around Oba-chan Yuki's shoulder and the other under her arm, holding and lifting her.

"Perhaps I should go back and lie down for a little while," said Oba-chan Yuki. "Could you help me? I am so sorry . . . to bother you."

"Oba-chan, this is not a bother. We are happy to help," replied Mama.

I wrapped my arms around Mama's waist, and the three of us swayed together for a moment.

"Mari, I will take Oba-chan back to her barracks. Could you run to the mess hall and get her a plate of breakfast and some hot tea with lemon? Go quickly and we'll see you back at her barracks, okay?"

I nodded and darted off for the mess hall, while Mama and Oba-chan Yuki headed back to her barracks. I ran as fast as I could and leapt up the mess hall stairs, passing the Clucking Sisters and their friends.

"Hey! No cutting in line! Come back here!" I heard one of them say.

I scrambled for a tray, plate, fork, and knife, then hopped in the front of the line.

"You must be very hungry," said an old man I didn't know. "Go right ahead."

I nodded thanks and held my plate out to the server.

"Well? Whatchoo want?"

I pointed to the powdered eggs and grabbed some toast.

"You gonna need some meat, too," he said. "Here." He plopped a couple of slabs of fried SPAM on the plate. My hat was sliding down over my face, and since my hands were full, I couldn't shove it back up, so I tilted my head back and smiled thank-you.

"Sure thing, ace."

I filled a cup with tea and a bit of lemon. I'd seen Oba-chan Yuki put a lot of sugar in her tea, so I dumped a bunch of that in too, then headed for the door. It was good that I kept my head up and eyes open, because just as I was about to skip down the stairs, one of the Clucking Sisters's friends stuck out her well-padded hip. I slipped round her and miraculously kept a majority of the tea in the cup, and the eggs, toast, and SPAM on the plate. As I scurried along the dusty dirt paths, I began to worry. I'd been to Oba-chan Yuki's barracks only once before, so I was a bit nervous that I'd get lost. Thankfully, Mama was standing outside waiting for me. She waved.

"Oh, well done, Mari. We'll go inside quietly. She may have fallen asleep."

Mama took the tray. Just as we were about to step inside, I looked over and saw that the window next to Oba-chan Yuki's door held one of those star flags. It was a small piece of white cloth with a red border. The cloth let everyone know that the family who lived inside had a son or brother or father in the army. Most of the time you'd see a blue star in the middle. On Oba-chan Yuki's piece of cloth the star was gold. A gold star meant that this family's soldier had died.

It was dark inside. I had to stop for a moment while my eyes became accustomed to the shadowy light. Mama put her hand on my back and guided me over to where Oba-chan Yuki lay in her bed. Oba-chan Yuki mumbled something. I couldn't make out what she'd said and looked up at Mama. She looked puzzled as well.

"What did you say, Oba-chan?"

"Inside my room," said Oba-chan Yuki. "It is dark. I am sorry if the darkness bothers you. I keep it this way for my eyes."

"Oh, don't be sorry," said Mama. "We're just fine. Aren't we, Mari?"

I nodded and smiled. When my eyes had become used to the darkness, I took a look around. The windows were draped with blankets.

"The sun hurts my eyes, you see, so I block the light with blankets," said Oba-chan Yuki. "My daughter, Eunice, says my room reminds her of a dark cave and I am her hibernating mama bear."

Oba-chan began to chuckle. Her laughing turned into a rasping cough. Mama helped her to sit up. She coughed some more and spat into a hanky that Mama held for her.

"Sorry. So sorry," she whispered. "As I said—the air is very thick today."

Mama took the plate from me and offered a forkful of eggs to Oba-chan Yuki.

"No, no eggs," said Oba-chan. "Just SPAM, please."

Mama cut a small piece of SPAM, a very small bite, and offered it to Oba-chan. She chewed and swallowed. This led to another round of coughing. But she was smiling while she coughed.

"Of course, I'd rather have some good broiled fish for breakfast. But we don't get that here, do we?" she said.

As Mama helped Oba-chan to some tea, I looked around some more. There was hardly any decoration, but on one wall I saw pictures and newspaper clippings and a big map. Nearby was a table, on top of which was what looked like a little religious shrine. There were candles, a statue of Mother Mary and another of the Buddha, a picture of a young man in an army uniform, a paper crane, and an army decoration. I took a closer look. The decoration was a ribbon with a medal attached. The medal was a purplish heart with a picture of George Washington in the middle of it.

I looked at the young man in the photo. He was wearing a uniform and looked to be older than Mak. There was a handwritten note beside the photo that read "June 1941." Where Mak looked friendly in his high school photo on Mama's bureau, this young man looked serious and fierce, like he was ready to fight. I couldn't imagine Mak ever looking like that.

"That is my grandson, Jack," said Oba-chan Yuki.

"A fine-looking young man. We are sorry for your loss," said Mama.

"Thank you very much," said Oba-chan Yuki.

Oba-chan pointed to a map on the wall. The word "Italy" had been written in red across the top and another, "Anzio," in the middle. There were tacks and colored string leading out from "Anzio," indicating something important, I guessed.

"Jack was very strong willed. Tough as nails, as they say. But Anzio was tougher," said Oba-chan Yuki. "Jack joined the army before Pearl Harbor. He worked very hard and became a sergeant. After the attack the army wouldn't let any Nisei fight. Had them cutting the grass, painting fences, and so forth. This infuriated Jack. It took quite a while for the army to change its mind. When it did, Jack went into combat with his battalion."

I didn't quite understand what she meant. I mean, I could see that Anzio was a town in Italy, a place by the ocean. That wasn't hard to figure out—I could see it on the map. But how could a place be tougher than a person? Do places pick on people? Fight with people? That just sounded a little crazy to me. I looked at Mama. She must've read my mind, as she often did.

"Oba-chan means that her grandson died at Anzio," said Mama. "There were terrible battles there."

"That is right," said Oba-chan Yuki.

I reached out to touch the little purple medal.

"No, Mari!" said Mama.

"Oh, it is all right," said Oba-chan Yuki in between sips of tea. "Go ahead, pick it up."

I picked up the little purple-and-gold medal with my thumb and pointer finger. It was heavier than I thought it'd be.

"Jack got that when he was wounded the first time, in April of this year," said Oba-chan Yuki, yawning.

I placed the medal in the palm of my hand. On the front was the picture of General Washington. Men look funny with their hair in ponytails. On the back were the words "FOR MILITARY MERIT" and Jack's name. It was a nice thing. I could see that Obi-chan Yuki was proud to have it, to have Jack remembered this way by the army. But I couldn't help thinking that I wouldn't trade a thousand of these for Mak.

"Mari," whispered Mama.

I looked up to see her holding one finger to her lips, and with the other hand she was pointing at Oba-chan Yuki. She was fast asleep. I could hear her breath—slow, rough, and raspy—but no more coughing. Mama lifted the tray from the bed and put it on the table nearby. I took her hand, and quietly we walked toward the door. Mama reached for the knob, looked back at me, and stopped.

"Mari," Mama whispered, "put it back."

I looked down at my hand and saw that I was still carrying the little purple heart! I couldn't believe it was still in my hand. I was so startled to see it there that I almost dropped it. Mama and I quietly walked to Oba-chan Yuki's little shrine, placed the medal on its tray and turned for the door. Mama opened it and we stepped outside. Before leaving, I looked back and saw that Oba-chan Yuki was awake and smiling at me. She winked, closed her eyes, and rolled over.

August 7, 1944
Camp Shelby
Dear Mari,

I hope you, Mom, and Pop are well and happy. Believe it or not, boot camp seems to suit me. Every day we march five miles out and five miles back through swamps and sweltering heat. All I've eaten here is SPAM, beans, turnips, and rice.

And yet—I've gained five pounds! Go figure!

We do a hundred push-ups anytime our drill sergeant thinks we're getting soft—which is just about all the time.

They must be pretty hard up for soldiers wherever they're going to send us! Boot camp ended last month, and ever since, they've been working us day and night on our duty assignment. You know I like cars and engines.

So I've put in to be a mechanic or a jeep driver for an officer.

The army is short on good mechanics, so I'm pretty certain of getting that duty assignment! A pal in my platoon has a Kodak camera. I'm sending you the picture he took of me and some friends in the motor pool. I'm the one covered in grease!

My pal Whitey Kurasaki has done so well in weapons training that they made him a unit leader. He can't wait to get to the front and fight Germans. I'm happy for him. As for me, I'm happy to do my part by fixing jeeps!

Please tell Mom that I'll be sending my pay back home again this month. There's not much to spend it on out here if you don't drink or play cards.

Okay, kiddo, it's just about lights-out here, so I'm going to sign off. Be good for Mom and Pop, and don't forget to give yourself some noogies!

Love, Mak

7. GOOD BONES

Just about every day over the next few weeks, Mama and I visited Oba-chan Yuki. We'd bring her breakfast, and afterward, if she was feeling okay, Oba-chan Yuki would tell us a story. I loved the stories she told about magical animals—like "The Singing Bird of Heaven" and "Tamamo the Fox Maiden." I'd draw while she told us the stories and show her the drawings I'd done when the story was over.

One morning she told us she had a surprise—her daughter, Eunice, the famous watercolor painter, was coming over to talk about art with me. Just after Oba-chan finished her fried SPAM and tea, we heard a knock on the door and in walked Eunice. She looked a lot like her mama—same size, small but wiry, and sort of weathered looking—but younger, of course. She smiled a lot too, just like her mama.

"This is my daughter, Eunice," said Oba-chan Yuki.

Eunice bowed and shook our hands. It was odd and a little funny to hear Oba-chan Yuki talk about Eunice as if she were still her little girl—especially since Eunice appeared to be about Mama's age. But Eunice didn't seem to mind. Whenever she turned toward Oba-chan, her eyes would crinkle and the sides of her mouth would turn upward into a warm smile.

I had brought my sketchbook with me that day, and after we sat for a bit, Oba-chan Yuki encouraged me to hand it over to Eunice for a look. Eunice took the sketchbook and sat quietly reviewing each drawing. She didn't say anything and spent a long time on each sketch. It made me uncomfortable—so much attention being paid to my drawings. It was as if she was giving my drawings the same kind of respect she'd give those done by a grown-up. Eventually she closed the book, looked up, blinked, and smiled at me.

"This is lovely work, Mari," she said.

I blushed. She opened my book again and pointed to one drawing I'd done of an archway that had been built in one of the Momoyama gardens in the camp.

"I know this archway. You have a good eye for the underlying structure of things. The bones of your drawing are very good. Your line work has a real assurance. And your page design is powerful. Reminds me of late Hiroshige prints. Impressive," said Eunice. "And she has had no other instruction, no other teachers in drawing?"

"We provided paper and pencils," said Mama. "Mari has done the rest."

Eunice looked again through my sketchbook, slowly flipping from page to page. Then she closed the book and looked directly at me.

"Mari, I am giving instruction in drawing and painting to a few children. They are all somewhat older than you, but I believe you have the skill to keep up if you want. If it is okay with your mother, I would like to invite you to join us. What do you say to that?"

I looked at Mama, then back at Eunice. I started bobbing back and forth in my chair. I knew that it looked strange, but I couldn't help myself—I was just so excited! Eunice liked my drawings! And not only that, she wanted me to join her drawing class with a bunch of older kids! I started to nod my head up and down very quickly.

"I think she likes the idea," said Eunice, smiling. "But what about you, Aki? Is this okay with you? It will cost some money for each class. Just enough to pay for supplies and a little left over for my time."

"Oh, yes," said Mama. "But you should know that Mari has chosen not to talk. At least not until her brother, Mak, returns from the war."

"Yes, my mother has made me aware of this. A vow of silence. Yes," Eunice replied. "I find her decision to be admirable. I would happily work with her regardless of whether she talks or not."

My heart was beating very fast. I was so happy, I began to clap. Eunice laughed.

"But, Mari," said Eunice, "I need to know if you will be willing to work. Are you serious about drawing?"

I could feel a cool tear sliding down my face. She was talking to me like I was a grown-up. It was an exhilarating and scary feeling. I gripped my hands together to steady myself, looked Eunice in the eye, and nodded once with determination.

"Good," Eunice said. "Your first class is this afternoon at the school. Bring your sketchbook and some pencils. I'll provide the rest. Let's shake on it."

She held out her hand and I shook it. Her shake was strong. Her hand dry and warm. What a great feeling! I thought we'd get up and leave at that point, but the grown-ups decided to hang around for a while longer, talking. I was so excited, I thought I might explode! I kept bouncing in my chair, looking toward the door every time I thought they'd finished blabbing. Eventually Eunice noticed my fidgeting and smiled.

"I think we better finish our talking before this little one bounces through the roof," she said. Mama laughed.

"One more thing," said Eunice. "I think it would help if I told my students about your not speaking and why. Is that okay with you?"

I thought for a moment and then nodded.

"Good. We'll see you at two o'clock at the front door of the high school," she said. "We'll work till about five o'clock and be finished before supper. Okay?"

I nodded happily and bounced out of Oba-chan Yuki's little cave-room and into the sunlight. We had spent quite a bit of time in there. Mama decided that we should just go straight to lunch. It didn't really matter to me if we ate now or never—I was just so excited about being invited to join Eunice's drawing class!

I have no memory of what we had for lunch.

On the way home from the mess hall, we stopped to pick up some of our laundry that had been drying on the line. Back at our barracks, Father had been reading his newspaper. He looked up as we entered.

I clapped my hands and then bounced like a rabbit over to his chair. Father folded his newspaper, put it on his lap, and crossed his arms.

"Why is she bouncing like this?" he said.

Mama told him all about Eunice's invitation for me to join her art class. Father placed his hands on my shoulders.

"I've heard of this Eunice. She is a very accomplished artist," he said.

I nodded and tried to do a little more bouncing, but Father added more pressure on my shoulders, holding me still.

"This is a great honor you've been given."

I nodded again and smiled.

"I hope that you will act properly," said Father. "I hope you will behave in a manner that will not embarrass yourself or your family."

Mama put down the laundry and stood beside me.

"She is just excited, Ichiro. That is all," said Mama.

"I know this, Aki," said Father. "But she is acting very silly just now, and I wouldn't want her to behave like this in class."

"She'll be fine," Mama replied.

I didn't know what to do. Mama and Father had been having more spats like this recently. Many of them seemed to be about me. I looked at Mama—she had moved over to a bureau to put some clothes away. Father was looking in the opposite direction. I put my sketchbook down, and then I did something I'd never done before. I took Father's hand in mine and I smiled at him. I wanted him to know that I'd heard what he'd said and that Mama was right, I would be fine. Father looked puzzled at first. He wasn't very fond of holding hands, either in public or private. But he must've understood, because after a moment he smiled back at me and nodded.

"Yes," he said. "This is an honor. And it is a confirmation of what we have known all along—that our Mari has talent!"

I looked over at Mama. She smiled and continued to put away the clean clothes. She was opening and closing the drawers very quickly. I had a feeling that maybe she was angry. Maybe angry at Father for the way he'd spoken to me. I couldn't tell exactly.

Later Mama encouraged me to lie down for a bit and take a nap, but I couldn't. I sat on the edge of my bed, my sketchbook in hand and four drawing pencils beside me. I thumbed through my drawings and thought about the things Eunice had said about the one I'd done of the arch in the garden. I hadn't really understood what she meant about it having good "bones." I didn't know drawings had bones. Unless, of course, it was a drawing of bones. But the more I thought about this, the more I wanted to run over to the high school and get the class started so I could learn more about "bones" and "structure" and anything else Eunice wanted to teach me about drawing.

"Come along, my little suzume," said Mama. "It's time for your art class."

I jumped. I'd been so intent on thinking about what

might happen at the art class, I'd forgotten the class was that afternoon. Sometimes that would happen—I would get so caught up by the idea of doing a thing that I'd forget to actually do it. But not today! I grabbed my sketchbook and my pencils and the hat Mak had given me and danced out the door behind Mama.

"Do well!" said Father as we left. I waved and smiled.

I wanted to run to the school, but Mama held my hand and told me that we had plenty of time. I was in such a good mood. I waved to people as we walked. I waved to people we knew and some we didn't know. I even waved to the Clucking Sisters. And they waved back! I was a little surprised by that but took it as more evidence of the magical nature of the day. And it felt like there would be more and even better magic to come! Drawing class!

When we finally got to the school, we found the front door was locked! I nearly screamed. Luckily, a teenage boy was standing just inside the door and opened it for us.

"You're Mari?" he said. I nodded. It was a solemn nod. I was doing my best to appear a little older.

"Hi, I'm Tomiche. You can call me Tom." He shook my hand and then Mama's. "I'm one of Eunice's students. We're just over there." He pointed to an open classroom door.

"Do you want to come and see?" said Tom to Mama.

I turned my back to Tom and, facing Mama, quickly shook my head no. This wasn't something I normally would've done. I usually wanted Mama with me anywhere I went. But just now I wanted to do this on my own.

Mama looked at me, smiled, and said, "No. I'm sure Mari will be fine. I'll be back at five o'clock."

I spun around and followed Tom into the classroom. In my haste, I forgot to say goodbye to Mama. When I looked back, she was gone. I felt a strange mix of sad and happy at the same time. But this lasted only for the moment it took me to step into the classroom.

Inside, the first thing I found myself looking at was a small pile of animal skulls sitting on a table in the middle of the classroom. Eunice was seated next to the table, a pencil in one hand and a razor in the other. There were five teenage students also arranged around the table—three girls and two boys. Eunice stood up, brushed some pencil shavings from her lap, and took my hand.

"Welcome, Mari. Let me introduce you to everyone," she said.

This was exciting! Eunice introduced me to each student. I shook their hands as we made our way around the table. The boys were Tom, of course, and Sadao and Hank. The girls were Tsuya, Flora, and Cho. They all seemed nice. Eunice pulled a chair over to the table for me, and we all sat down.

"Mari," said Eunice. "I've told everyone that you won't be speaking and why. They understand and support you in this. Let's give Mari some applause."

Everyone clapped. I bowed a thank-you and blushed. This was very odd. All I'd done was walk in the room, and people were clapping for me. I didn't know what to do, so I stared at my shoes and continued blushing.

One of the girls, Cho, leaned over toward me. "My brother is in the army too," she said.

"And my uncle," said Hank.

"By the way," whispered Cho, "I like your hat."

I smiled and looked down at my feet. I felt grateful for their understanding but also uncomfortable at all the attention. I took out my pencils and put them on the table. I could see that everyone else had their own pile of pencils as well. Most had four or five, but Hank must've had about a dozen.

"Ah, good, Mari," said Eunice, looking at my pencils. "These are fine-quality drawing pencils. Good HB leads. And a nice 2B. Excellent. Let's talk a little about the proper way to sharpen a pencil."

She walked back to her chair, took a seat, picked up her razor and a pencil. She looked at the point of her pencil and smiled.

"Very dull—the point, that is, not the subject matter," she said, smiling.

I looked at the point. It didn't look dull to me.

"To normal people, sharpening a pencil is a thing that they do without thinking. They see their pencil is dull. They stick it into a mechanical pencil sharpener, and after a crank or two it's more or less sharp. But not us, right? Why? Because we're not normal—we're artists. We're abnormal!"

She laughed at this. So did everyone else. I didn't have the slightest idea why this was funny. It was as if she was saying that all artists were abnormal and that this was a good thing. I must've mistaken what she'd said. A good thing to be abnormal? Father'd have a gigantic fit over that.

"We pay close attention to the points on our pencils. We like to keep them sharp. And when we sharpen them, we don't use one of those clumsy mechanical pencil sharpeners that spin around and around while you turn a little handle. Instead we use a very, very sharp razor."

Eunice placed the pencil in her right hand, positioned it over an old piece of newspaper on the table, and, with the razor held between the thumb and pointer finger of her other hand, whittled a small sliver of wood and lead from the pencil's tip. She turned the pencil a fraction and did the same thing again several times. I noticed too that as she pushed the razor forward with one hand, she was also gently pulling the pencil back with the other.

I looked around and saw that everyone except me had picked up their pencils and razors and begun the sharpening process. I picked up mine and thought I'd just start chipping away. But it wasn't as easy as it appeared. The razor was probably sharper than any knife I'd ever used in the kitchen. I was a little frightened by it.

"Cho," said Eunice, "could you give Mari a little guidance? We don't want her to cut herself."

Cho came around the table and stood by me.

"Are you left handed or right?" she said.

I raised my left hand.

"Me too!" she said. "Okay then, you'll hold the pencil in your right hand and the razor in your left. Like this."

She held the pencil and razor just as Eunice had, except

with a slight difference—she placed her right thumb on the back of the razor, perhaps to give herself a little more control of the movement. Slowly she turned the pencil and chipped, turned and chipped. She didn't say a thing. She would just stop and then show me the little ways in which she was accomplishing the task. I looked up at the other students for a moment. They all seemed to be sharpening their pencils in the same way Eunice had, except each was just a little different.

"There," said Cho. "Now you give it a try."

I took my pencil and razor from her and held them as she had directed. I even placed my thumb on the back of the razor as Cho did. Slowly and with concentration I applied pressure to the razor, pushing it forward slightly with my left hand and pulling the pencil back gently with my right. A sliver of lead and wood slid away from the pencil's point and landed on the table. This small result was very satisfying, more satisfying than I'd expected.

"Good," Cho said to me, and to Eunice, "I think she's got it."

"Very good," said Eunice.

Cho turned to head back to her chair but stopped and leaned toward me.

"I really like what you're doing about your brother and the army," she whispered. "I imagine it's not easy. And not talking must drive your parents nuts. I wish you could talk so you could tell me all about it."

I smiled. Cho was nice. I continued whittling my pencil. It didn't take long for me to start to feel frustrated. Every time I got it to a fairly nice point, I'd whittle a little too far and snap the point off. This happened three or four times on the same pencil. In the process I'd whittled about half of the pencil away. I looked up to see that everyone else had just about finished whittling their pencils.

"Let's get busy drawing," said Eunice. She saw the stub I'd made of the one pencil I'd been whittling and smiled. "Don't worry, Mari, you'll get the hang of it soon enough. Let me help for now." She took my pencils and quickly whittled each one to a perfect point.

"Now," continued Eunice, "I'd like everyone to turn your gaze to this lovely pile of skulls we have here before us. Aren't they lovely? We have Tsuya and Cho to thank for gathering them during their walk in the hills last week. Let's give them a little applause."

Everyone clapped. Sadao raised his hand and then pointed to one of the larger skulls.

"Oh, yes! And Sadao, too," said Eunice. "He also brought in a few skulls. Including this big one. A coyote, Sadao?"

"Yes, I think so," he replied.

"Let's give Sadao some applause too," said Eunice.

More applause. There was a lot of applauding in this class. This seemed odd. Applause for bringing in a skull? I mean, all this clapping was fun, but most teachers I'd known didn't encourage this sort of goofing around. Fun and work didn't go together in a normal classroom. But here we were, doing work and laughing. I don't know, maybe this was how artists got things done. Or maybe it was just how Eunice ran her class. Work and fun—I liked it. But it made me feel odd, too.

"We should have enough," said Eunice. "So everyone grab two. Oh, and let Mari have the two biggest skulls. It'll be easier for her to start with larger objects."

Everyone leaned over the pile of skulls. Sadao picked up the bigger coyote skull he'd brought in and put it in front of me.

"Be careful of the teeth," he said. "They're really sharp." He held up a finger and I saw there was a bandage on it. We exchanged smiles.

Cho picked up another one of the bigger skulls and handed it to me. "I think it's a buck jackrabbit. Just look at those two front teeth."

"Those are called incisors," said Hank, indicating the front teeth of the jackrabbit. "And the pointy ones on the coyote skull are called canines."

"Hank is the smartest person in the room," whispered Tsuya as she walked behind me. "At least, that's what he'll tell you."

Everyone made their way back to their seats.

"Please choose one of the skulls to draw," said Eunice. "Look at them both and select the one that is most interesting to you. Don't spend any time worrying about which one to choose. It's okay to select the one that simply catches your fancy."

I looked closely at the coyote skull on the table in front of me. I'd never looked at a skull close up before. There were little holes all over it. And cracks that, upon even closer inspection, looked less like cracks and more like tiny rivers zigzagging back and forth across a map. Some of the bone was very thick. Other pieces, especially near the nose, were almost paper thin.

"Good," continued Eunice, "now place the skull on your desk, near the window. Set it so the light falls across it and casts a shadow."

I put my coyote skull near the window. The sunlight was very bright, and the skull cast a crisp blue shadow.

"Now come on over to where I am and let me show you what method we'll focus on today. That's good," she said as we gathered around her. "Watch what I do."

Eunice looked at the skull for a moment, then gently placed the tip of her pencil on her paper and began to draw. I watched her hand flow smoothly across her paper. It was very quiet and I could hear the sound of her pencil as it made its mark. The image of the skull was slowly taking shape, and as it did, I noticed something strange—Eunice wasn't looking at what she was drawing! Not at all! Her gaze stayed locked on the small skull, and not once did I see her look at her paper to check to see if what she was doing was good or if it even looked like a skull!

I examined her drawing more closely. It wasn't the most accurate drawing I'd ever seen. There were parts of the skull that seemed as if she'd put them where they shouldn't be. But, somehow, the attention she'd given to the details—the thicks and thins of the lines she made, and the way they described the delicate edges of the skull—these things kept me fascinated. It was strange, because usually I liked drawings that showed things just as I thought they should be, just as they might look in a photograph. But it was the lovely lines she was making that kept me glued to her drawing. I felt entranced by the movement of her hand and wanted her to continue drawing for the rest of the afternoon, but she abruptly stopped.

"There," she said, assessing her drawing. "Good enough, eh? Now, who can tell what approach to drawing I used in this sketch?"

Everyone but me raised their hand. Eunice chose Tom.

"It's a contour technique drawing," he said.

"Good," replied Eunice. "And, Tom, what are some of the guidelines regarding contour drawing?"

"When we draw using the contour approach," said Tom, "we look for the edges of things. All things have edges. Even a strand of hair has a contour."

"Good," said Eunice. "Now, can anyone tell me anything else about contour drawing or the way I created this sketch?"

I raised my hand. I guess I was just so excited that I'd forgotten that I didn't talk. I had a lot of things that I wanted to share. I wanted to say that I'd noticed that Eunice hadn't looked at her drawing while she was making it. I wanted to say that usually I didn't like drawings or paintings that didn't look like a photograph, but that I really enjoyed this drawing. I wanted to say that I'd been enchanted by the way she'd made the thicks and the thins with her pencil. So many things to say!

"Mari," said Eunice, "do you want to talk?"

I shook my head no.

"But you have something to say?"

I nodded. How could I say what I wanted to say? I paused,

then stood, leaned forward, and pointed at Eunice's eyes.

"You noticed something about my eyes?" said Eunice.

I nodded. Then I made a quick movement with my hand, indicating a connection between her eyes and the skull. I nodded vigorously, *Yes!* Then I pointed again at her eyes, but this time I followed that by pointing at her drawing and shaking my head, *No!*

"Hmmm . . . ," said Eunice, "I don't quite get what she's saying here."

There was a momentary silence. I pointed at Eunice's eyes and her drawing and shook my head again. Someone must understand what I was saying!

"Oh, I know!" blurted out Cho, standing as she did so. "She's saying that she noticed that you looked at the skull when you drew the sketch and not at the drawing itself!"

Eunice looked at me expectantly. "Is that right, Mari?"

I nodded again, then plopped down on my chair, happy to have been heard and just a bit exhausted from the effort.

"Well then—good job, Mari and Cho!"

Cho put her hand out toward me and we shook.

"Yes, that is an excellent observation, Mari," said Eunice. "I didn't look at my drawing—well, perhaps I did take a few peeks—but as you noticed, I spent most of my time with my eyes on the skull. This is how we develop a stronger eye-hand connection. Well done, Mari. Applause for Mari and Cho."

"Miss Eunice," said Sadao, "you forgot the 'mind and heart' thing you told us last week."

"Oh, yes," replied Eunice. "Thank you, Sadao. Hmmm . . .

the mind and the heart. Another reason we sometimes practice looking more at the object that we are drawing than at the drawing itself is because our minds, while very helpful in most situations, can actually get in the way of a good contour drawing. The mind can be very critical. Too critical sometimes. And if we spend too much time looking at the drawing we are making, our mind will step in and remind us over and over just how incorrect our drawing is. Have any of you experienced this? An overly critical voice in your head telling you that your drawing is terrible?"

I was surprised to see everyone raise their hand. I thought I was the only one with an unkind voice in my head telling me that my drawings stunk. I'd thrown away many of my drawings because of that nasty voice. And what was worse, sometimes that voice was so convincing that I'd stop drawing altogether for a while.

"Well, you see," continued Eunice, "we don't want to completely ignore the critical side of our minds—but every once in a while it's good to just focus on the object we are drawing and let the drawing be just as our heart and hand want it to be. So this is why we look less at the drawing and more at the object and learn to celebrate whatever surprises we find when we complete the drawing."

Eunice looked at her watch and jumped up.

"Oh goodness—I've done so much talking today! It's already three thirty, and I'm the only one who's done any drawing. Let's get back to our places."

I looked at the coyote skull and thought, *How am I going*

to draw this thing without looking at my drawing? Eunice had made it look so easy. She just stuck her pencil point on her paper and started moving it around, and—*poof*—she'd made a beautiful drawing. It seemed far too easy. It was still hard to accept that she'd not looked at her drawing.

"Having some difficulty?" said Tom.

He was sitting on the opposite side of the table from me and must've noticed that I was staring at my blank sketch pad.

"Best thing to do is just start drawing," he said. "And don't worry about mistakes. We all make them."

"Yep, he's right," whispered Tsuya. "Even Eunice makes mistakes. I've seen her make some doozies."

I turned to look at her, puzzled.

"It's true," said Tsuya. "Everybody thinks that teachers like Eunice are these perfect people who are as wonderful as they are because of some kind of magic or because they have special genes or something. Fact is, they are good at what they do mostly because they made mistakes, lots of 'em, and didn't stop. She learned from her mistakes and just kept drawing. That's all."

Tsuya smiled without looking at me. I noticed that she'd continued drawing all the time she was talking to me and hadn't taken her eyes off the skull in front of her. I turned back to my drawing, put my pencil point on the paper, and thought, *Just draw. Just push the pencil.* But I still couldn't get myself to draw the way Eunice had.

"I tell you what," said Eunice. I jumped. She'd been standing behind me and I hadn't noticed. She put her hand on my back. "Sorry. Didn't mean to startle you. But I tell you what—you just go ahead and draw that skull whatever way feels comfortable to you. Don't worry about this contour drawing method for now. Just draw the way that feels right to you. Okay?"

I gulped and smiled and nodded my head.

"Good," she said, and moved on to another student.

Truth be told, I didn't really want to draw the skull. I suppose it was an interesting thing to draw, but it was also creepy. All those sharp coyote teeth—I mean canines. I was staring at the skull, trying to figure out what part of it I could draw that wasn't so creepy, when a sparrow landed on the sill outside the window. It sat there for a moment, looked at me and, I think, looked at the skull, and flew off.

I knew right then what I would do. First, I started drawing the sparrow from memory. Then I drew the skull but showed only a part of it, and I placed that part in a lower corner of the paper. I tilted the sparrow's head and had it looking out of the corner of its eye at the skull, and I drew the sparrow's shadow. The shadow flowed across the sill and the table and up onto the brow of the skull. Then I smeared the lead in the shadow, blending the lines and smoothing the texture. It looked pretty good.

I'd used all the pencils and so picked up the shaving razor and began whittling. I was so intent on evaluating the drawing that I wasn't really watching what I was whittling—nor did I notice that I'd cut myself. But Tom did.

"Hey," he cried, "she's bleeding!"

I looked up to see who it was that Tom was talking about

and saw that he was pointing at me. Then I looked down at my sketch pad. There were drops of bright red on my drawing! I thought for a moment, *Hey, who's been bleeding on my drawing?* Then I realized it was me. The razor was so sharp that I hadn't even noticed what I'd done. Everyone rushed over.

"Oh dear!" said Eunice. "Let me see."

I gave her my right hand.

"Ah, the pointer finger. All right, we'll need to wrap it up and get you over to the hospital. Might need a stitch or two."

She took a piece of paper towel from a nearby sink and wrapped my finger.

"Hold it tight, now. Let's go."

I stood, wobbled a bit, and steadied myself.

"She's looking unstable, Miss Eunice," said Hank. "I can carry her."

Eunice had taken my arm and was walking with me to the door.

"Oh, for crying out loud, Hank!" said Tsuya, holding the door open for us. "The hospital is right next door. Every time somebody gets a bump or a scrape, you want to pick them up and carry them someplace."

"I'm an Eagle Scout," said Hank. "I've been trained for this sort of thing."

"Thank you, Hank," said Eunice, "but I think we'll be all right. Class is done for today. Would you all mind getting things put away here? We'll meet next week, same time."

"Sure thing," said Hank.

Eunice and I scurried across the sandy courtyard between

the high school and the hospital. She'd placed one arm around my shoulder, and her other hand was holding mine.

"I think you're being very brave, Mari," said Eunice. "Are you usually this brave?"

I smiled at her and shrugged. I wanted to tell her that, even though I did feel a little dizzy, I really wasn't feeling any pain. What was concerning me most was the response this would get from Father. My cut finger, the blood, drawing skulls—this would all most likely qualify for the category of abnormal. I fully expected him to have a fit about this, too. And in spite of my cut finger, and any confusion or frustration I'd felt about some of what she was teaching, I wanted more than anything to come back to Eunice's drawing class the next week.

Inside the hospital, a nurse looked at my finger.

"Hmmm," she said, "I don't think we need to wait for the doctor. He went into town to pick up some supplies."

She cleaned the cut, applied some disinfectant.

"Was it a new razor? Not an old, rusty thing?" she asked.

"Brand new," said Eunice.

"Ah, good. She won't need a tetanus shot. I don't think she'll need any stitches, either. A nice clean cut like this just needs a good butterfly bandage."

For a moment I thought the nurse was going to bring out a box of bandages made with or by butterflies. But that wasn't the case. She put some hydrogen peroxide on my finger—that stung—then some gauze, and then she applied a bandage that looked a little like a butterfly when she was done.

"There," she said, looking satisfied. "You keep that clean and dry for the next few days, then come back for a change of bandage. Or sooner if it starts to turn red or itch. Okay?"

I nodded.

She handed me a small envelope. I could feel pills inside. "Aspirin for tonight. It'll probably start to ache just before bed." The nurse patted my shoulder, then reached into a cupboard and took out a basket. Inside the basket were cherry lollipops.

"Courage deserves a reward," she said, smiling.

I reached into the basket and pulled out two—one for me and one for Eunice.

"Thank you, Mari."

Eunice and I walked together back to my barracks, our lips lollipop red. It was late. Mama greeted us at the door, worry wrinkles around her eyes.

"Tom told us what happened. Are you okay?" she said.

I nodded, hugged her, and showed her my butterfly bandage. Mama told us that Tom had also brought my sketch pad and pencils back from the high school.

"He is a good boy," said Eunice.

"Upon hearing about your injury, Father immediately ran out looking for you," said Mama. "He must've taken the long way around to the hospital."

After a bit I heard his boots stamping up our barracks stairs. The door swung open. "Mari!" he cried.

Father put his hands on my shoulders and looked at my head. "I don't understand!" he said. "Her skull is not cut. There is no cut on her head."

I showed him my bandaged finger.

"But . . . but the young man said 'skull.' He said, 'Her skull is cut.' I remember him saying this!" said Father.

"You ran out before he finished telling us what happened," said Mama. "He said that she was drawing a skull and cut her finger while sharpening her pencil."

"Her finger? Not her skull?" said Father. He stepped back, found a chair, and sat down. "Oh. Oh. I've run all over camp. I'm tired."

"Just a small cut on her finger, Ichiro," said Mama. "Mari will be fine."

"Yes," said Father. "A hurt finger is better than a cut skull."

Eunice coughed. "I must apologize," she said. "It is my fault that Mari cut herself today. I should've been paying more attention."

I shook my head. *No,* I thought, *it's not your fault! It's mine. Don't give Father a reason to stop me from going to your class.*

"In addition to being gifted, Mari is a good student," continued Eunice. "I would like to be given the chance to continue teaching her. But I will understand if you don't wish that to happen."

No! I wanted to scream. *You're a good teacher. It's my fault. I won't do it again!* I sat down on the edge of my bed, put my face in my hands, and began to cry.

"This is good of you to say," said Mama. "It has been a trying evening. May we discuss this and let you know later?"

"Of course. Good night."

I didn't hear Eunice leave. When I looked up, I saw that she was gone. Mama was talking quietly to Father. She had poured some warm water from the teapot on the heater onto a cloth and was wiping his face. I was so angry, I kicked the floor. They looked at me.

"It's been a long day, Mari," said Mama. "I think you should get to bed early tonight."

I kicked the floor again, rolled away from them onto my bed, and continued to cry. No more Eunice. No more drawing lessons—all because of a stupid little cut on my finger. I woke sometime in the middle of the night. I'd been grinding my teeth. I could tell in the darkness that Mama and Father were both asleep because of their breathing. I looked at the butterfly bandage on my finger and noticed that it seemed to glow in the cool blue light of the moon. I knew that I'd never be able to re-create that cool blue glow with just the black lines and gray tones that came from a lead pencil. I'd need to learn to paint in color. And I knew that, no matter what, I would continue to learn from Eunice.

August 20, 1944
In transit
Dear Mari,

I hope this letter finds you, Mom, and Pop in good health. You'll be happy to hear that I've been made a corporal! That's right—I've got two stripes on my arm! I've been bumped up a pay grade too! I'll be driving a jeep for an officer. I'm tickled pink about it.

I'm sorry I've taken so long to get back to you. We got our orders to ship out not long after we finished our duty assignment training. Things were pretty disorganized for a bit. It was "Hurry up and wait" and then "Go! Go! Go!" until they marched us over to the train depot. Then it was more "Hurry up and wait" until our train arrived.

It took us forever to get everyone on the train.
They packed us so tight, we could hardly move.

We were greeted by USO girls at every station with coffee and doughnuts.

YOU THREE ARE RIDICULOUS.
KRISTEN MICHELLE! YOU COME BACK HERE!
HEY, FELLAS!
ANYBODY WANT A DOUGHNUT?

SAY, WHERE YOU BEEN ALL MY LIFE?
RIGHT HERE. HANDING OUT DOUGHNUTS TO GI'S.

STEP BACK! WE'RE PULLING OUT!

I'M IN LOVE! WAIT FOR ME!
C'MON KAZ-- SHE'S NOT GOING TO WAIT FOR YOU.
GOOD LUCK, FELLAS!
BE QUIET, MAK. I'M TALKING TO MY FUTURE WIFE.

OUTRAGEOUS.
SHAMELESS!
HAVE YOU EVER?!

Not much else to report here except that I can't wait to get off this train and stretch! I may never sit down again. Please tell Mom and Pop I'm thinking of them. I'm saving up noogies for you when I get home.

Love, your big brother Mak

8. RED ROVER, RED ROVER

A week passed. Not one word was said about Eunice. Or my going back to her drawing class. Not one! I did my best to get them talking on the subject, but Mama and Father focused themselves on their chores or the newspaper or something else. Anything but me.

One night found us trudging to the mess hall through a windstorm. As we entered the hall, I noticed my reflection in the door's small window. I looked like a dark-haired piece of pastry that'd been dusted in cinnamon. We stood at the door for a moment, slapping and wiping as much of the dust from our clothes as possible. At our table, Mama and Father stared at their food and there was no talk between them. I ate quickly, then sat with my hands folded in front of me. Beside my tray were my sketchbook and a pencil. When Mama and Father happened to look in my direction, I made sure I had a pleasant smile on my face. I hoped that by acting politely, I might convince them to allow me to continue to study with Eunice. No such luck. After Father finished the last of his tea, he placed his cup back in its saucer and noticed my sketchbook.

"Aki, what is that doing here?" he said, indicating the sketchbook. "I thought we agreed there'd be no more of that."

"No more of what, Ichiro?" replied Mama.

"No more drawing. I thought we agreed she was done with drawing."

"We agreed that Mari would stop attending Eunice's drawing class while her finger healed and then we would decide about further classes," said Mama quietly. "But we did not agree that she would stop drawing."

Father's nostrils flared while he took a deep breath. He looked around the room. It seemed as if he was looking for someone to help him win the argument. Then he took another deep breath and looked down.

We continued to sit, Mama quietly looking at her untouched dinner, Father grumbling to himself and glaring at his empty teacup, and me staring at my bandaged finger. It ached. I thought of the moment when I'd cut myself and wished myself back to that time. If only I'd put down the razor blade. If only I'd asked for help. If only I'd . . . It was useless. No matter how many ways I might "if" myself out of the situation, it wasn't going to change anything now. I'd just have to wait and see what would happen once my finger had healed.

"Come, family," said Mama, rising. "We have babies to attend to."

We walked together to the Children's Village, but not arm in arm. By the front door some men were pulling tumbleweeds away from the building. Father left us to help the men. Mama and I entered to find some of the children playing red rover in the central hall. "Oba-chan Aki!" one of the children cried, and grabbed Mama's hand, pulling her into the game. I continued on toward the baby room and found Keiko sitting in the lap of a nurse on the floor. Keiko was crying as if she was hurt or perhaps someone had taken her favorite toy. I sat down beside them.

"She's been like this since they started playing red rover," said the nurse. "You know how much she loves to play. But she's too small and will get hurt playing with the bigger kids."

I reached for her, but she turned away, wailing. I got an idea and crawled across the room, turned toward them, and opened my arms.

"Red rover, red rover, send Keiko on over!" I shouted.

Keiko stopped crying and stared at me. Then she gulped, clapped her hands once, and screamed with glee. After scrambling down from the nurse's lap, she crawled across the floor, laughing all the while, and dove into my arms. We cheered for her for a bit and she laughed like crazy. After a moment's rest the nurse hollered, "Red rover, red rover . . . ," and before she finished, Keiko was crawling across the floor toward her. We did this over and over, so many times that I lost count. Keiko was one very happy, tired baby when I gave her a nighttime bottle. She was fast asleep before she'd even taken half a dozen gulps.

It wasn't till Mama, Father, and I were walking home that I realized I'd broken my vow of silence. At first I was angry at myself. How could I have forgotten to stay silent?

But then I thought that if a vow of silence couldn't be broken now and then, especially to make a sweet baby laugh, then it wasn't worth being a vow in the first place. I said a quick prayer for Mak, hoping that would mend any damage I'd done to the vow, and kept on walking. Along the way I practiced making drawings in my mind, drawings of Keiko crying, Keiko laughing, Keiko crawling. Practicing drawing in my brain wasn't as satisfying as actually drawing something, but it was better than not drawing at all. Back in our barracks I sat on my cot and drew in my sketchbook. I filled three pages with happy Keiko drawings. I did this until Father blew out the light.

As I lay on my back, staring at the cracks in the ceiling, I yawned once, twice, and felt a small pain in my chest. Not a big pain. Just a small one. But it was there nonetheless. I was also having a little difficulty breathing. Nothing serious. I thought of Oba-chan Yuki saying the air was thick. *Probably just the dust,* I thought, and forgot about it.

As I fell asleep, I remember wishing that Keiko were there, living with us, and not an orphan in the Children's Village. I could take care of her. I could. I knew how to make her happy. I knew how to make her feel loved. I would take good care of her if they would let me. But I knew this was a silly wish. Grown-ups don't let kids take care of kids. They should, but they don't.

9. NOT LIKE IN THE MOVIES

I'd guess that most people don't die the way they do in the movies. At least, Oba-chan Yuki didn't. One day she was there and the next she wasn't. Nobody made any speeches. No big orchestras playing sad, sad music. There were no big crowds standing around outside her room, crying. There was just her family and me and Mama. It wasn't fair. There should've been much more.

Mama and I had continued to bring Oba-chan Yuki breakfast just about every day. Some days she would cough a lot and complain about the air being too thick again. Other days she would seem like she was on the way to being much better, laughing and joking with us.

One hot, dusty morning Mama opened the door to Oba-chan Yuki's barracks. I was carrying a tray with her breakfast.

"Good morning, Oba-chan!" said Mama cheerfully.

Oba-chan Yuki didn't respond. She didn't move.

Mama touched her shoulder and called her name again. No words. No sound. I thought she was just deeply asleep. Nothing unusual about that. But she wasn't sleeping. I didn't know it then, but Oba-chan Yuki was dead.

Mama knew it, though. She didn't say anything, but she knew. She had me put down the tray, took my hand, and walked us toward the door. I felt confused—why didn't Oba-chan wake up? Why were we leaving?

"Come, Mari," said Mama as we headed out the door.

She walked quickly, holding my hand. She was holding it so tightly that after just a little while it began to hurt. I pulled my hand away and stopped. Mama turned to me and tried to grab my hand again. I could see she was crying.

"Please, Mari," cried Mama, "come along! This is important."

I got scared. My knees felt wobbly. For some reason I decided that sitting down on the dirt was a good thing to do. So I did. And then I started to cry too. I didn't really know why I was feeling so strange. Well, maybe some part of me knew, but most of me still didn't understand. Mama sat down beside me in the dirt. She put her arm around me and we sobbed together for a bit.

"I am sorry," whispered Mama. "I'm sorry, Mari. I should have told you. We are going now to the hospital barracks. We are going there because I think our Oba-chan has died, and we need to get the doctor. I'm sorry."

Some men saw us sitting in the road and came over. They thought we'd fallen down and were hurt. Mama told them what had happened and what we'd been doing. One of them ran off to the doctor's, and the others stayed with us. I stood up but felt very dizzy. I wobbled a bit, and one of the men picked me up. I don't remember much after that.

I woke up later in my bed. Mama was there. And Father.

And one of the doctors from the hospital barracks. Everything felt very heavy. I couldn't lift anything—not the blankets, my arm, or even my eyelids. I couldn't lift the washcloth off my forehead. I drifted in and out of sleep while the doctor was there. They talked to one another in very serious whispers. I remember him saying something about "croup" and "We might need to order penicillin."

"She may have pneumonia," whispered the doctor. "Whatever it is, it has been made worse by the dust storms. I would move her to the hospital, but honestly, I think she'll do better here with you. Keep her warm. Give her lots of fluids. The next few days will be crucial."

"But I don't understand. She's not been ill. How is it that she is suddenly so sick?" said Father.

"I don't have an answer for that. I just know that she has these symptoms and we must treat her for them," replied the doctor. "I'll be back later. Good night."

Mama spent every minute with me for those first few days and nights. I remember eating lots of cabbage soup and drinking a lot of lemon water, so much that I thought I was going to explode. I used to like lemons. Not anymore.

Sometimes I had a high fever. I had a lot of crazy dreams, too. For instance, I remember dreaming that I was the sparrow and that I was flying around looking for my sparrow village after my tongue had been cut out by the farmer's wife and her sister. And yes, the Clucking Sisters had found their way into my dreams. I was very happy to wake up from that one.

Later I started worrying that maybe it was my fault that Oba-chan Yuki had died. If I'd just spent more time with her or made her drink as much lemon water as I was, then perhaps she'd still be alive. Thankfully, one night Mama told me that Oba-chan had died from the pneumonia because she was old and that I'd lived because I was young. It was that simple, she said. I'm glad she told me that. It didn't make me miss Oba-chan any less, but I stopped feeling like her dying was my fault.

It may seem silly, but I was pretty proud of the fact that I still kept my vow of silence through all of it. I didn't even talk when I felt the most sad for Oba-chan Yuki. It was important to me that I stay silent so I could keep my vow. Mama told me that I'd talked a little in my sleep when I had the high fever. But that wasn't my fault—I was asleep.

The doctor found my not talking pretty odd. One night he shared this concern with Mama and Father. I knew that he and Father would become the best of friends when I heard him whisper that he thought my behavior was a little "abnormal." Mama smiled, thanked him, and escorted the doctor out the door.

September 1, 1944
Embarkation center
Dear Mari,

I was very happy to receive your letter and to learn that your finger is on the mend. No more goofing around with sharp stuff for you! We finally made it to our new camp. I can't tell you where it is, but just know that we are about as far east as you can go and not be swimming in the Atlantic.

WHITE
MEN
COLORED

HEY, LIEUTENANT. PERMISSION TO GO TO THE LATRINE?
YEAH, BUT BE QUICK ABOUT IT.
YES, SIR.

WHITE
MEN
COLORED

From the train station they marched us over to our new camp. It felt good to stretch my legs.

Things picked up as soon as we got into camp. First we dropped our gear in our barracks, then we lined up for a bunch of shots. My arm looked like a pincushion.

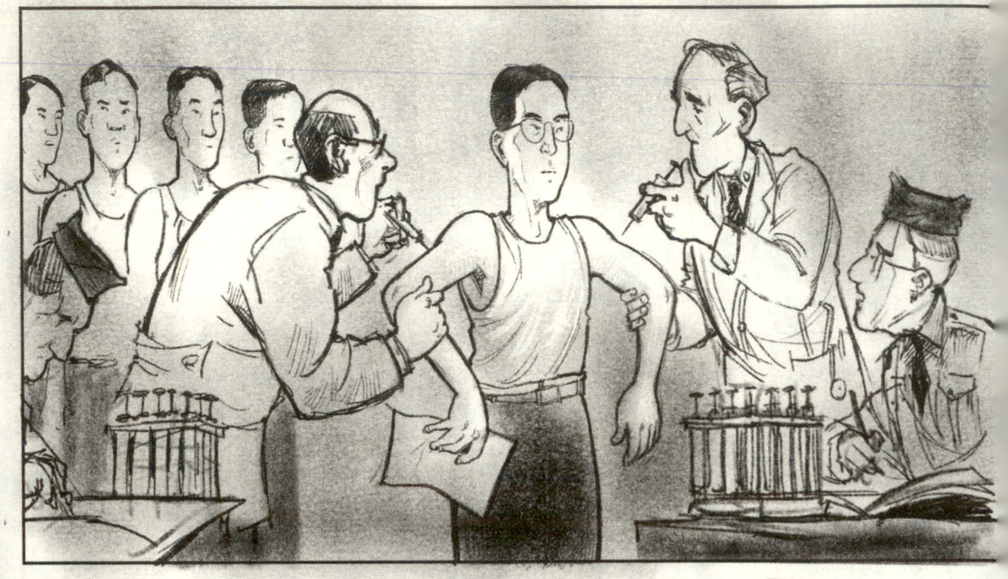

On our second day in camp we received gas mask training. Let me tell you, I'd rather wear a wool sweater in July in Manzanar than be strapped into one of these smelly masks all day.

YES, SERGEANT.
OUTSTANDING.
PAY CLOSE ATTENTION TO THE MANNER IN WHICH THIS SOLDIER APPLIES HIS MASK.
HEY, WHITEY-- YOU'LL PROBABLY GET MORE DANCES AT THE USO CLUB WITH THAT MASK ON THAN OFF.
VERY FUNNY, SMART GUY.
THAT'S GONNA CATCH YOU A BEATIN'.
HEY! D'YOU TWO KNUCKLEHEADS WANT TO SPEND THE REST OF THE WAR WEARING ONE OF THESE WHILE YOU DO KP DUTY?
NO, SERGEANT.
GOOD.
NOW SHUT YER YAPS AND PAY ATTENTION BECAUSE THESE INSTRUCTIONS MAY JUST SAVE YOUR LIVES!
IS THAT CLEAR?
YES, SERGEANT.

That'll have to be it for now. I'm about to pull guard duty, and I need to put a shine on my boots. It amazes me how much time I spend shining my boots in the army.

Love, your big brother Mak

"Mari," said Mama one evening as she and I ate some cabbage soup together in our room, "a friend would like to visit with us."

I put my spoon down and looked at Mama.

"It's Eunice. She wants to sit with us and talk about Obachan Yuki. Would that be okay with you?"

I nodded.

"Good. She'll be here soon."

Not long after, there was a light knock at our door. Mama answered it. Eunice entered. She smiled at Mama and bowed. Then she smiled at me. It gave me a pleasant warm feeling inside just to look at her.

"Please excuse my coming so late."

"Oh, please, don't worry. We are happy to see you. Would you like some tea?"

"No, thank you. I will only be a moment," said Eunice. "Hello, Mari. I'm happy to see that you are feeling better."

I smiled. Mama brought two chairs over to my bed, and they sat.

"Still not talking, eh?" said Eunice. "Good for you."

We sat in silence for a while, perhaps for only a second or two, but it felt longer. Eunice smiled at me again, then patted my hand.

"Listen, Mari, I have a favor to ask." She reached into her coat pocket and pulled out a small box. "You gave my mama, Yuki, some very happy moments in the last days of her life."

Eunice looked down at her folded hands. Slowly she opened them. Inside was a little box. She opened the box, and inside that was the purple heart medal.

"I . . . my family . . . would like to ask if you would keep this Purple Heart for us—to remember our Jack and the friendship you had with our mama, Yuki. Would you do that for us, Mari?"

I nodded, then put my head against Mama's shoulder and cried. I couldn't look at Eunice. I couldn't look at the Purple Heart. I just felt so sad about the whole thing—about Jack dying at Anzio and about Oba-chan coughing and dying and about how far away Mak was. I felt Eunice pat my hand again. I heard the scratching noise that a chair makes when it's pushed back, then I felt the little box being put into my hands.

"Thank you, Mari," said Eunice. The door clicked shut behind her.

The next morning I pinned the Purple Heart to my hat. But that seemed too show-offy. Then I pinned it to my jacket lapel. But that didn't feel right either. Father made it clear that he thought the best place for it was sitting safely inside its little box in my sock drawer. I didn't like that idea at all. Later I pinned it on the inside of my jacket. This way I could wear it and think of Oba-chan Yuki without making a show of my feelings. And that's where it stayed for a very long time.

Later that week we learned that Eunice and her family had applied for and gotten a travel waiver. Mama told me that they were leaving for good, that they'd soon be on a train to Chicago. They were not the first of our friends to receive permission to leave the camp. Others had started to leave much sooner. As long as internees had some white person to vouch for them and were moving away from the coast, the government was happy to get families out of the camp. We hadn't applied for a waiver because Father didn't like the idea of having to move east and insisted that we would wait till after the war to move back home to Florin, California.

Eunice came to see me on the morning that she and her family were leaving. It was very early and I don't remember much of our goodbye. I was still pretty weak from being sick. Later that day I even wondered if perhaps her visiting me to say goodbye had been a dream, but then Mama gave me the note she'd written to me.

Dear Mari, read Eunice's note, *I regret that I won't be able to watch you and your talent grow, but I encourage you to keep drawing. You have a wonderful gift, and I hope that you will continue to share this gift with all of us. Perhaps we will meet again. Until then, I will keep you in my heart. Sincerely, Eunice.*

I opened my sketchbook and tried to do a drawing. Nothing came out of me but scribbles. I turned to the drawing I'd done in Eunice's class. A sparrow, a shadow, a skull, and some red drops. *What a stupid drawing,* I thought. I wanted to tear it up but didn't. I closed the sketchbook. I didn't draw again for a long time.

10. IS THIS A PRIVATE FIGHT?

One night Father came into the barracks while Mama and I were doing a little cleaning up. I was feeling better, but I still wasn't allowed to run around outside, so it was decided that doing chores would be just the right sort of exercise for my continued recovery. Parents—where do they come up with these ideas? Luckily, it was summer. Otherwise I'm sure they would've had me doing homework, too.

Father was hiding something in his jacket and had a big smile on his face. I think I even heard him chuckle.

"Good evening!" he said.

This was not like the Father I knew.

"Ichiro," said Mama, "what's wrong?"

"There is nothing wrong," replied Father. "Why do you think something is wrong?"

"Well," said Mama, "you have a big smile on your face. And you seem very . . . happy."

"I don't understand. These are good things."

"It's just that we don't see you like this very often. It is . . . abnormal," said Mama, smiling.

Father looked at me. I smiled back and was grateful

that he'd come to accept that I wasn't going to talk, because this meant I wouldn't be required to get involved in what seemed like a tricky conversation. He turned back to Mama.

"Aki, I still don't understand," he said. "However, that is no matter. What is important is . . . this!" He pulled an envelope from his jacket.

"A letter!" said Mama. "Is it from Mak?"

"Yes! And it is to me."

"How nice, Ichiro! I told you he would write back to you!"

"Yes, you did. And yes, he did! Would you like me to share it with you?"

"Oh, yes!" said Mama.

I bounced on the bed and clapped my hands. Father brought two chairs over. I flopped down on the bed. Mama took my hand, and we listened while Father read Mak's letter.

September 20, 1944
Embarkation center
Dear Father,

I hope this letter finds you all in the best of health. Well, I finally got a look at the Atlantic while on a march today. It looks just like the Pacific—big, blue, and wet. I didn't get to see much of it, though, because my view was blocked by all the ships being loaded with supplies.

We marched down to the docks and past some Liberty ships. I've never seen so many tanks and guns in one place!

Tonight we get a little downtime. Me and my pals Whitey and Kaz plan on attending the USO club's enlisted men's dance.

HEY, MAK, YOU THINK THEY'LL HAVE DOUGHNUTS?
SURE, I DON'T SEE WHY NOT.
I SURE HOPE SO.
SORRY 'BOUT THAT. PARDON ME, MISS.
DON'T MENTION IT.
HEY, WATCH WHERE YOU'RE GOING, NIP!
HE APOLOGIZED, RICK. LET IT GO.
NO WAY!
I'M GETTIN' SICK OF THESE LITTLE NIPS MUSCLING IN ON OUR GIRLS.
C'MON, WHITEY. LET'S GET SOME FOOD.
PLEASE, RICK. DON'T START ANYTHING! YOU PROMISED.
YOU SHOULD LISTEN TO THE LADY AND BACK OFF, PAL.
I AIN'T YOUR PAL.
SHORTY.

SAY, IS THIS A PRIVATE FIGHT OR CAN ANYBODY HAVE A PIECE OF IT?
STAY OUTTA THIS, PUNK!
RICK! LISTEN TO ME!
WHAT'RE YOU LOOKIN' AT, HAOLE?
SEE NOW, THAT KINDA TALK AIN'T GONNA MAKE YOU ANY FRIENDS.
C'MON, LET'S GET OUT OF HERE, WHITEY.
STRIPES ON A JAP. LIKE A BOW TIE ON A MONKEY.
WHAT'D YOU SAY?
WHO YOU CALLING PUNK, SHORTY?
RICK! YOU PROMISED!
I SAID--OOOF!
NEVER MIND!
Smack!
I HEARD YOU THE FIRST TIME!
LET'S GET OUT OF HERE, WHITEY!
NOT NOW! I'M BUSY!

MP'S!

LEMME GO!
I AIN'T FINISHED!
C'MON, WHITEY! THE MP'S ARE HERE!
TIME TO GO, BOY!
WHAT'D YOU PULL ME OFF THAT HAOLE FOR?!
I WAS WINNING!
YOU SHOULDA LEFT ME BE!
YOU COULD JUST SAY "THANK YOU," Y'KNOW. WE PROBABLY JUST SAVED YOU FROM A COURT-MARTIAL.
BOY DON'T KNOW WHAT'S GOOD FOR HIM.
LOUSY, STINKIN' HAOLE!
YOU GOT TO COOL DOWN, BRUDDAH. SAVE THE FIGHT FOR THE NAZIS.
WHY? WHAT'S THE DIFFERENCE BETWEEN THESE PUNKS AND THE NAZIS?
GOOD QUESTION.

If you don't hear from me for a while, you'll know that I'm on a boat heading across the ocean. Again, I can't say exactly where.

I just got word that we're moving out tomorrow to catch a Liberty ship across the pond! Look out, Adolf, here we come!

Don't worry about me, Pop. Like I said, I'm just a jeep jockey for an officer. It's a cushy assignment, and most likely I'll be spending my days miles behind the lines. Give my best to Mom and Mari. I'll get a letter off to you as soon as we make port.

Love, your son Mak

11. GETTING MY WINGS

It's a scientific fact that grown-ups are much nicer to kids when we're sick. Take the Clucking Sisters. You've seen just how nasty they've been. Well, not long after I got pneumonia, they started showing up at our barracks with desserts and candy and whatnot. They sat with Mama and clucked about the camp gossip. They smiled at me and patted my head and ate the goodies they'd brought. It was nice enough, I guess, but it seemed odd because they'd been so mean before and now they were acting so nice. Who can understand grown-ups?

Then there were the grown-ups who I didn't know all that well but who were extra nice to me when I was sick. Mr. Tayenaka was one of those. One day he knocked on our door. Mama let him in and they spoke for a moment, then Mama introduced us. I knew his name but had never met him. He was known around the camp for making toys for kids out of the spare pieces of wood he found. Mostly he made airplanes for boys.

He smiled at me, bowed quickly, and reached inside the bag he was carrying. From it he pulled something wrapped in old, yellowed newspaper. I took it from him and unwrapped the paper. Inside was a small carving of a bird. It was a sparrow! Its wings moved back and forth, and its little mouth was open like it was singing. It was wonderful! I thanked him, nodding my head and bowing. He bowed too, then backed away. He seemed very shy. Mama walked him to the door and he left.

"Oh, it's lovely!" said Mama as she came to sit beside me. "Such detail. This is very special."

I held the little wooden bird up to the light. Mr. Tayenaka had carved it in such a way that I felt like I was looking into the face of an actual sparrow. I placed it on my little night table and looked at it till it was time for my nap. I wondered how he'd been able to put so much sparrowness into a piece of dead wood he'd found lying in the dirt somewhere in the camp.

It was midafternoon. Mama had promised that tonight I could go to the mess hall for dinner. This was the first time since I got sick. Her one condition was that I take a nap beforehand. As I lay in bed, I thought about Mr. Tayenaka's gift.

I woke up, having had a dream about the wooden sparrow. I dreamed that it was trying to talk to me but it couldn't because it had a cough. It kept spitting up wood chips and choking on its broken tongue. I shook my head and jumped out of bed. As I put on my shoes, I realized that I'd already begun to forget the dream. I grabbed my drawing pad and made a quick sketch. I'd finish it later.

Mama and Father were at the door with their jackets on. I reached for the little wooden sparrow on my night table. Before I tucked it into my pocket, I looked at its little face—its eyes, its open beak—and I noticed that a little notch had been cut into the bird's tongue. Funny, I hadn't seen that before.

12. BABY MEDICINE

The trip to the mess hall for dinner had gone well. I wasn't tired and I didn't start coughing. So Mama and Father thought it all right for me to visit Keiko. I'd been asking to see her since I started feeling better. Right after supper we visited the Children's Village.

I hadn't played with her in weeks, and I was worried that Keiko might not remember me. But that was silly. When I went into the baby room, I saw that she was standing by herself. All by herself! When I'd last seen her, she had been very good at crawling but not too good at standing. But there she was, standing and bouncing to a baby song that was playing on the phonograph.

I clapped my hands and she spun around. She smiled and waved, then lost her balance and sat right down with a thump. She was laughing as she fell but started crying the second her bottom hit the floor. I think she was more shocked than hurt. I ran over, sat on the floor, and put her on my lap. I started to bounce her up and down. She giggled a little and then hugged me. There's nothing like a good hug from a happy baby.

We played for a while that night. Then I helped get her ready for bed—got her dressed in her nightgown and gave her a bottle. She fell asleep in my lap while I fed her. I picked her up and put her into the crib. I remember looking at her for a moment. Her face so sweet and calm, her mouth open a little, her arms flung wide like she couldn't wait to wake up and give me another hug.

I went to play with Keiko every afternoon for the next few days. And every night after dinner I would play with her and put her to bed. Mama told me that babies can be the best medicine. I didn't think about it then, but I know that taking care of Keiko was the best thing for me. I felt better every day.

And then Keiko was gone.

I don't like talking about this part.

One day I was happy and Keiko was happy and everything was fine. And the next day—she was gone. They sent her to live with a family in Detroit who had adopted her. They didn't even let me say goodbye to her.

The nurses told Mama that they didn't want to upset me or Keiko. They thought it best to send her off without us getting all worked up about it beforehand. They were wrong. Mama thought so too.

They should've let us say goodbye.

13. *LES ENFANTS ET LES TRAÎTRES*

I got sick again after they sent Keiko away. The fever flared up again too. I did a lot of sleeping. I don't remember much about this part.

Oh, there was one thing—we got a letter from Mak. He arrived at the war.

October 7, 1944
Dear Mari,
Hello from France! I apologize for not writing sooner. Letters will be more forthcoming now that I'm on dry land. The voyage was a bit choppy at times, but we've arrived no worse for wear and tear. Got a good look at the Rock of Gibraltar, then made a quick stop in North Africa. Then we sailed across the Mediterranean and made port in southern France.
WELCOME TO FRANCE, BOYS. I HOPE YOU'RE FEELING REFRESHED AFTER OUR DELIGHTFUL OCEAN VOYAGE.

BONJOUR, LES ENFANTS.

YOUR LEFT. YOUR LEFT. YOUR LEFT, RIGHT, LEFT.

CORPORAL KAZUO!
GET YOUR UGLY BUTT BACK INTO FORMATION. PRONTO!
BON APPÉTIT, MON AMI.

HERE I COME, SARGE!
WHAT DO YOU THINK YOU'RE DOING?!
TRYIN' OUT MY FRENCH ON LES ENFANTS!
MOVE IT, YOU KNUCKLEHEAD!
BOY, YOU PULL ANOTHER STUPID STUNT LIKE THAT AND I'LL BUST YOU BACK TO PRIVATE SO FAST YOUR PEA-SIZED BRAIN'LL POP!

I've been doing my job as an officer's jeep jockey. He's an aide to the regimental commander.

WHAT'S IN LYON, SIR?
WELL, I'LL TELL YOU, MAK--WE'VE GOT OURSELVES AN IMPORTANT ASSIGNMENT.
WE'VE GOTTA LINE UP A FIRST-CLASS HOTEL FOR THE GENERAL TONIGHT. THE OLD BOY'S VERY HAPPY ABOUT THE REGIMENT'S SUCCESSES UP NORTH AND WANTS TO CELEBRATE!
Y'KNOW, I'D LIKE TO GET TO KNOW YOU BOYS A LITTLE BETTER.

Driving a jeep isn't the most important job, but every little bit helps. I'm so happy I studied French in school. It comes in handy in navigating the roads.
MIND IF I ASK YOU A QUESTION?
NOT AT ALL. GO RIGHT AHEAD, SIR.
JEEPERS, NOW THAT I'VE GOT THE CHANCE, I'M FEELING A LITTLE BASHFUL.
HEH, HEH.

OKAY, WELL, HERE GOES. I'VE ALWAYS WONDERED ABOUT YOUR EYES.
NOT JUST YOUR EYES, MAK, BUT ALL JAPANESE EYES. YOU ALL HAVE THAT EXTRA PIECE OF SKIN ABOVE YOUR EYE.
YOU KNOW-- THAT PART THAT MAKES YOUR EYES SLANTY.
I ALWAYS WONDERED IF IT GOT IN THE WAY.
AW HECK, THIS IS SO EMBARRASSING, BUT DOES IT EVER...
I HOPE YOU DON'T MIND MY ASKING. I'M JUST CURIOUS AND I'VE NEVER HAD THE OPPORTUNITY TO ASK.
UNDERSTOOD, SIR. WELL, I WEAR GLASSES BUT I SEE JUST FINE. HOW 'BOUT YOU, HARRY?
I SEE PRETTY GOOD.
TRAÎTRES! TRAÎTRES! TRAÎTRES!

UM.
WELL, UH...
...MAKE IT HARD TO SEE?
YOU'RE SURE? IT DOESN'T GET IN THE WAY AT ALL? NOT EVEN A LITTLE BIT?
NOT AT ALL, SIR.
NOPE.
WELL, THERE YOU GO. YOU LEARN SOMETHING NEW EVERY DAY! DONCHA?
YES, SIR.

WELL, WHAT DO WE HAVE HERE?
LOOKS LIKE THE RESISTANCE HAS ROUNDED UP SOME MORE COLLABORATORS.

MP
MP
J'AI COLLABORÉ AVEC LE BOSCHE
TRAÎTRES EN FRANCE

WHAT'S THAT SIGN AROUND HIS NECK SAY, MAK? YOU UNDERSTAND THEIR LINGO. CAN YOU READ IT?
IT SAYS HE DID BUSINESS WITH THE GERMANS.
J'AI FAIT DES AFFAIRE AVEC LES BOCHES

We're moving around a lot, but I will do my best to keep on writing. I may only be able to get a note to you every now and then. But please know that you, Mom, and Pop are always on my mind. And I don't want you to worry about me. This war looks like it'll be over soon. In fact, most of the fighting seems to be over long before I get there. Take good care of Mom and Pop.

Love, your big brother Mak

14. GO HOME

School started a few weeks ago. Mama has let me stay with her for now, doing chores. I still haven't been feeling so good. I guess I should be going to school, but I just don't feel good. Not so much sick, I guess. More like everything has turned boring or gray or something. I don't know. Everything just makes me tired. The idea of watching other kids play or listening to kids laughing gets on my nerves. It just makes me feel more tired.

Maybe if Keiko were still here, things'd be all right. But she isn't. Mama told me the orphanage is sending all the babies away for adoption. They want to get them adopted before the camp closes. Everybody says that the war is going so well that it will probably be over by Christmas. Then the camp'll close and everyone will go home. That'd be good, of course. Then Mak could come back. But where would we go? Our farm is gone. Mama says they won't want us back there—not in our town, not even in California. We don't have a home.

I don't know. I'm just tired.

10/10/44

Dear Mari,

We're moving fast now. From what I've been able to see, France is a beautiful country.

C'MON, KAZ. THERE AIN'T GONNA BE NO BABY IN THERE.
YOU'RE RIGHT. NOBODY HOME.

C'MERE, BOY. I'M NOT GOING TO HURT YOU.
LOOK AT YOU TWO. WORRYING ABOUT BABIES AND STRAY DOGS. A COUPLE OF FIERCE FIGHTING MEN, YOU ARE. WHAT AM I GONNA DO WITH YOU?

HUH, WHAT'D I SAY?
FRENCH DOG. PROBABLY DOESN'T UNDERSTAND ENGLISH.
HA. GOOD ONE, KAZ.
C'MON. LET'S KEEP MOVING. I'VE GOT GUARD DUTY IN THIRTY MINUTES.

HOLD UP THERE, BOYS.
WHAT'S UP, SARGE?
WELL, WE GOT A VERY TRICKY SITUATION UP AHEAD.

MP
THERE'S AN UNEXPLODED BOMB IN THE REMAINS OF THAT BUILDING. MEANWHILE, WE GOT SOME CIVILIANS TRAPPED IN THE BASEMENT. AND THAT THREE-STORY WALL AIN'T LOOKING TOO STEADY. GOT SOME SPECIALISTS DOING WHAT THEY CAN, BUT IT'S GONNA BE TOUCH AND GO FOR A WHILE YET.

SORRY, BOYS. YOU'LL NEED TO TAKE A DIFFERENT ROUTE HOME.
NO PROBLEM, SARGE.
WE BETTER SCRAMBLE, WHITEY.
OR YOU'RE GONNA BE LATE FOR GUARD DUTY.
HEY, HOLD UP. YOU MEN ARE WITH THE 442ND REGIMENT? THE ALL-JAPANESE GO FOR BROKE BOYS? RIGHT?
THAT'S RIGHT. WHAT ABOUT IT?
EASE UP, WHITEY.
THIS HAOLE IS MUCH BIGGER THAN YOU, TOO.
THAT'S AN MP.
BE QUIET, KAZ.
I CAN SEE THAT.
JUST SAYIN'.

BEEN HEARING SOME MIGHTY GOOD THINGS ABOUT YOUR OUTFIT. MIGHTY GOOD. THE 442ND'S A GOOD UNIT TO HAVE AROUND WHEN THINGS GET HOT. YOU MEN STAY SHARP UP ON THE FRONT. YOU HEAR?
THANKS, SARGE. WILL DO.
WELL, THAT WAS A LITTLE CONFUSING. HUH, WHITEY?
WHAT WAS CONFUSING?
DON'T WIND HIM UP, MAK. OLD WHITEY GONNA SNAP.
THAT MP WAS A HAOLE AND HE SEEMED LIKE A DECENT GUY.
WAIT! YOU THINK I HATE ALL HAOLE! DONCHA?!
I TOLD YA NOT TO WIND HIM UP.
SEEMS LIKE IT. SOMETIMES.
WELL, I DON'T!
YES, YOU DID.

I DON'T HATE ALL HAOLE!
I JUST HATE THE ONES WHO THINK THIS IS THEIR WORLD AND WE'RE JUST THE HELP!
YOU HEAR ME?!

YOU HEAR HIM, MAK?
OH, YEAH.
ME TOO.

I wish I had more time to write, but I don't just now. The regiment is racing north and it's all we can do to keep up. I hope you're being good for Mom and Pop. Give them my best. Give yourself a hug for me.

Love, your big brother Mak

15. MAK'S FACE

I was thinking about Mak the other day, and I couldn't remember what his face looked like. When I tried to remember fun times we'd had together—like our first winter in Manzanar, when it snowed and we had a snowball fight—I just couldn't see his face. I could remember his hands and the jacket he wore and the hat he had on. But no matter how hard I tried, I couldn't see Mak's face. I know that sounds crazy, but that's the way it was. Of course, we had pictures of him. All I needed to do was look at one of them. I guess I was just having trouble seeing him in my mind.

I hope he can still see my face.

I hadn't been able to sleep well. When I lay down at night, I'd look up at the ceiling and try to make drawings out of the cracks in the ceiling. Some people count sheep to help them get to sleep. I make drawings out of the cracks in the ceiling. It usually worked, too, but lately the drawings I'd make out of the cracks were all sad ones: sad Mak or sad Oba-chan or sad Keiko. Rather than falling asleep, I'd start to get agitated and roll around. Sometimes Mama would hear me and wake up. Being Mama, she was usually pretty nice about it. But nobody likes to get woken up from a sound sleep one night after the next.

"Are you okay, Mari?" Mama yawned, leaning on her elbow.

I nodded.

"Can I do anything for you?"

I shook my head.

"You tell me if you need anything."

Dear Mama. I smiled and gave her a thumbs-up. Mama was soon back asleep. I could tell by her snoring. Mama's snores sounded like a big cat purring, interrupted now and then by little coughs.

I lay there, unable to sleep. Looking out the window, then back at the ceiling, then the window. I was getting very agitated. So I slipped out of bed, grabbed my sketch pad and pencils, and tiptoed out the door. Once outside, I sat down on the stairs and leaned my back against the doorframe. It was a clear night. The stars shone so brightly, like they all had something to say and wanted to be the first to say it.

I sat there for quite a while, waiting for the stars to figure out who'd talk first. I don't know what time it was when I went back inside. But I do remember that I had been shivering. When I got back in bed, the shivering continued. When it finally stopped, I noticed that I was sweating. I put my hand to my head and found that it was a bit hot. My fever was back.

10/18/44
Dear Mari,
I hope you are all doing well. How is school? Has it cooled off there yet? I am fine and all is well here. My outfit just got orders to move out. Some of us will be leaving sooner than others.

YOU KNOW THE DRILL, MAK.
THIS ARMY DON'T BELONG TO YOU. IT BELONGS TO UNCLE SAM. WE DO OR DIE AND WE DON'T TRY TO FIGURE OUT WHY.
C'MON, WHITEY, STOP MISQUOTING THE ARMY MANUAL TO ME.

BESIDES, YOU'RE MISSING MY POINT.
K-RATIONS
ALL RIGHT THEN, WHAT'S YOUR POINT?

LOOK, ALL I'M SAYING IS--BE CAREFUL.
YOU GET INTO ALL KINDS OF TROUBLE WHEN I'M NOT AROUND, SO DON'T DO ANYTHING STUPID UP ON THE FRONT LINE.

AW, LOOKIT YOU GETTIN' ALL SENTIMENTAL ON ME.
YOU'RE GONNA MISS OL' WHITEY. AIN'T YA?
STOP GOOFING AROUND, WHITEY. I'M SERIOUS.

I MEAN IT, WHITEY. DON'T BE A HERO UP THERE.
I HEAR YOU, BRUDDAH. OL' WHITEY GONNA BE ON HIS BEST BEHAVIOR TILL HIS MAMA MAK ARRIVES.
NOW LET'S GO GET US SOME CHOW.

Almost all my friends have shipped out. I'm going to be one of the last of my company to leave camp. Guess my jeep driving is just too important to risk sending me too close to the front.

SIR, IF YOU WOULD JUST--
YOU KNOW, MAK, YOU ARE STARTING TO GIVE ME A SEVERE PAIN IN THE BUTT.
I'M SORRY, SIR, BUT--
SHUT UP, CORPORAL. THAT'S AN ORDER.
YES, SIR.
EVER SEEN ONE OF THESE BABIES, PRIVATE FUKUHARA?
YES, SIR. THAT'S A GERMAN PISTOL. A LUGER.
YOU'RE DARN TOOTIN' SHE IS! I BOUGHT IT FROM A DOG-FACE COMING OFF THE LINE WHO SAID HE TOOK IT OFF AN SS OFFICER. I'M GONNA MAKE A MINT ON THIS WHEN I GET HOME.
PRETTY SCARY STARING DOWN THE WRONG END OF ONE OF THESE, AIN'T IT, PRIVATE?
UH... Y-YES, SIR!

DON'T WORRY, PRIVATE.
I'M NOT GOING TO SHOOT YOU. I TOOK THE AMMO CLIP OUT.
UH, YES, SIR.
BUT DID YOU CHECK FOR A ROUND IN THE...
BLAM
...CHAMBER?
ZING
THUNK

WHAT WAS THAT?!
WHAT WAS IT?!
A SNIPER! TAKE COVER!
GIMME A TARGET AND I'LL TAKE HIM OUT!
DID ANYBODY SEE WHERE IT CAME FROM?
OOPS.

GRAB SOME DIRT, BOYS, UNTIL WE LOCATE THE SNIPER!
EXCUSE ME, SIR, BUT NOW MIGHT BE A GOOD TIME TO PUT THAT PISTOL AWAY.
UH, YEAH. GOOD IDEA.
STAY DOWN, BOYS!

I have to sign off now, but I'll write every chance I get. Keep sending me your letters and beautiful drawings, too! Be good for Mom and Pop. And stop getting sick, okay?

Love, your big brother Mak

16. FEATHERS FOR MY WINGS

I didn't tell Mama about the fever. Over the next few days it seemed to come and go as it pleased. And I never got too hot or had those crazy shivering spells like when I was really sick. So I just kept it to myself. I kept my sleeplessness to myself too. Soon it became a habit for me at night to wait for Mama's snoring to start, and out I'd go to sit on the front steps. I'd sit out there for hours, sometimes almost till sunrise, and then head back to bed. Not long after, I'd start the day with Mama and Father as if everything were fine.

Of course, I walked around all day like an exhausted zombie. Sometimes Mama would notice and ask if everything was all right. I'd smile and keep on drawing or whatever it was I was doing. This seemed to satisfy her. I didn't know it then, but all of this—the sleeplessness, the fever, the worrying and sadness—was leading up to something.

One night when I'd actually been able to get to sleep after Father put the light out, I had some bad dreams. I don't remember them. But I do remember waking up feeling confused and frightened. I thought about nudging Mama, talking to her, but didn't. Instead I got up and walked outside. I didn't pick up my sketch pad. I didn't sit on the stairs. I picked up the wooden sparrow, went out the door, and walked through the camp, up one dusty dirt road and down another. It seemed like everyone was asleep but me.

The dirt felt good on my bare feet. I held the wooden sparrow at shoulder height, and with my other arm extended, I pretended that we were flying together. After a while—I don't know how long—I found myself standing by the old camouflage factory. There was a little breeze, and the camouflage was blowing about. It looked almost like the building was a big bird and it was flapping its wings, trying to take off. Thinking about that made me laugh.

I reached up to touch the camouflage, and a thought came to me. *I could wear some of this and I could be a bird too.* It was a silly thought, I know. But it seemed like fun. So I grabbed at the camouflage and pulled at it. A big strip of it tore away and fell on me. There must've been a nail in it or something, because as I drew it over my head and around my shoulders, I felt something scrape at my forehead. But I didn't mind. I just wanted to arrange my feathers and hurry home to show Mama. She was going to love seeing her little suzume wearing new feathers. I guess this all sounds kind of crazy. But it didn't feel crazy at the time.

When I got back to our barracks, the sun was beginning to rise. I opened the door and looked inside. Mama and Father were still asleep. I did my best to slip back in without waking them, but my feathers knocked over a cup on our table and Father sat up.

"Mari? What are you doing?" said Father.

I smiled at him and flapped my wings.

Father swung his feet to the floor. "What have you got all over you? Aki, wake up!"

Mama sat up, rubbed her eyes. "Mari, is . . . is that camouflage?" she said.

I flapped my wings again.

"Look at her head, Aki!" said Father. "She's bleeding!"

Mama sat on the edge of their bed. "Mari, come here. Let me look at you."

Father stood. "She is filthy!"

Mama hugged me and stroked my head. I smiled.

"Help me pick her up, Ichiro. We've got to get her to the hospital and get this cut looked at."

Father reached forward and started to pull at my new feathers. I screamed. Not like a girl, of course, but like a suzume.

"Peep! Peep, peep!"

"Ichiro!" cried Mama.

"But this stuff is filthy! It may have bugs."

"Stop picking at her and help me get her to the hospital!"

Father carried me all the way to the camp hospital. Mama was right beside us. I flapped my wings the whole way.

10/22/44

Dear Mari,

I hope you and Mom and Pop are well. I am in good health. I have been very busy these past few days.

LISTEN UP, LIEUTENANT. THE KRAUTS HAVE CUT OUR PHONE LINES TO BRUYÈRES AGAIN. I WANT YOU TO GO UP THERE, GET A STATUS REPORT FROM THE UNIT COMMANDER, THEN GET YOURSELF BACK HERE PRONTO AND REPORT WHAT YOU'VE FOUND. UNDERSTOOD?
YES, SIR.
GOOD. NOW GET MOVING, LIEUTENANT. I NEED THAT STATUS REPORT ON THE DOUBLE.
REGIMENTAL HEADQUARTERS
BRUYÈRES ISN'T TOO FAR FROM HERE.
YEP. THAT'S WHAT I HEARD.

EXCUSE ME, SIR. PERMISSION TO SPEAK?
WHAT ARE YOU STILL DOING HERE? DIDN'T I TELL YOU TO GET MOVING?
SIR, YES, SIR. BUT I...
I JUST WANTED TO POINT OUT THAT ASSIGNING ME TO COURIER DUTY IN AN ACTIVE COMBAT ZONE WOULDN'T BE THE BEST USE OF MY EXTENSIVE TRAINING AS A LIAISON OFFICER.
NOW YOU LISTEN TO ME, YOU LITTLE PIP-SQUEAK!
YOU JUST TAKE YOUR "EXTENSIVE TRAINING" UP TO BRUYÈRES AND YOU FIND OUT WHAT IS GOING ON UP THERE AND THEN YOU GET BACK HERE DOUBLE QUICK OR, SO HELP ME, I'LL ASSIGN YOUR SORRY BUTT TO A FRONTLINE COMBAT PLATOON.
UNDERSTOOD?!
Y-YES, SIR.
GET ME THAT STATUS REPORT. PRONTO!
YES, SIR.
AND I BETTER NOT FIND OUT YOU SPENT YOUR TIME IN SOME CAFÉ ALONG THE WAY!
YES, SIR. I MEAN NO, SIR.

I'm sorry for such a short note,
but we're on the move again.
I'll write as soon as I can.
Love, your big brother Mak

Mama told me later that when we reached the hospital, my fever had spiked to 103 degrees and I really started to have a fit. They wanted to give me an ice bath to bring the fever down, but they had to get me to calm down first. So I was given a shot of medicine. I don't remember any of it. But I do remember the dream I had when I finally fell asleep.

In the dream, Mak and I were back inside the camouflage factory. The sun was shining so brightly and there were so many swallows flitting about. Everything was so clear and sharp. I could see everything, right down to each tiny feather on every little sparrow as it flitted by. And I remember thinking, *This isn't a dream. This is real.*

As Mak and I walked around, we kicked up clouds of dust from the floor. Mak put out his tongue to taste it. "Try it," he said. "It tastes like cinnamon." I thought he'd gone crazy, but then I remembered our first winter at Manzanar and him encouraging me to catch a snowflake on my tongue. That had been a lot of fun. So I stuck out my tongue. We hadn't had any cinnamon since we'd been put in Manzanar, and I didn't really know what to expect. But that first taste was something else. Even now I still don't know how to fully describe the feeling that came over me as the fine powder coated my tongue and the smell and taste of cinnamon poured into me. I just remember feeling like it was almost too much, like I'd gotten everything I'd ever wanted and didn't know what to do with it. Or something like that.

I heard a baby laugh and looked to my left to find a bear who looked like Oba-chan Yuki sitting on a purple heart medal about the size of a big tree stump. On Oba-chan's lap sat a little red puppy who looked like Keiko. She was wearing a dog collar with a tag that said RED ROVER. In their hands they held wooden spoons, and they were helping themselves to a large bowl of cinnamon dust. "Better than roasted fish for breakfast!" said Oba-chan.

The last thing I remember was looking back over at Mak and seeing that he'd picked up a musical instrument, like a little guitar. The guitar was orange with purple polka dots. Mak was trying to play it but wasn't doing well. I came closer and soon found out why. His fingers were sausages. That's right. Sausages. He looked up at me, smiling, and said, "If you can have a kabocha head, then I can have sausage fingers."

I know it sounds crazy, but it all made sense in the dream.

10/23/44
Dear Mari,
I may not be able to write for
some time, so I will get a
quick note off now. I've
traveled so far and seen
so much in just the past few days.
Someday I will tell you all about it.
But right now I'm just too busy.

SIR! BRUYÈRES IS JUST DOWN THAT ROAD. WE'RE ALMOST THERE! ALL WE GOTTA DO IS GUN THE JEEP THROUGH THE INTERSECTION AND WE'LL BE PAST THE SNIPER BEFORE HE EVEN KNOWS WE'RE GONE!
THE GENERAL SAID NOTHING ABOUT ENGAGING THE ENEMY IN THIS ASSIGNMENT. I WILL NOT RISK MYSELF OR MY MISSION BY RECKLESSLY VENTURING INTO A DANGEROUS SITUATION.
THIS IS A COMBAT ZONE, SIR. EVERY PART OF IT IS DANGEROUS.
DO NOT LECTURE ME, CORPORAL. WE WILL STAY PUT UNTIL THAT SNIPER HAS BEEN ELIMINATED.

GO BACK! GO BACK! SNIPER!

GET OUT OF
HERE! YOU'LL DRAW THE
SNIPER'S FIRE!

HEY! YOU IN
THE AMBULANCE!
HEY!
WAKE UP IN THERE! YOU'RE
GOING TO DRAW THE
SNIPER'S FIRE!

YOU! IN THE AMBULANCE!
I'M TALKING TO YOU!
MAKE HIM SIT DOWN, MAK.
YOU'RE FORGETTING THE SNIPER, SIR.
MOVE THAT TRUCK!

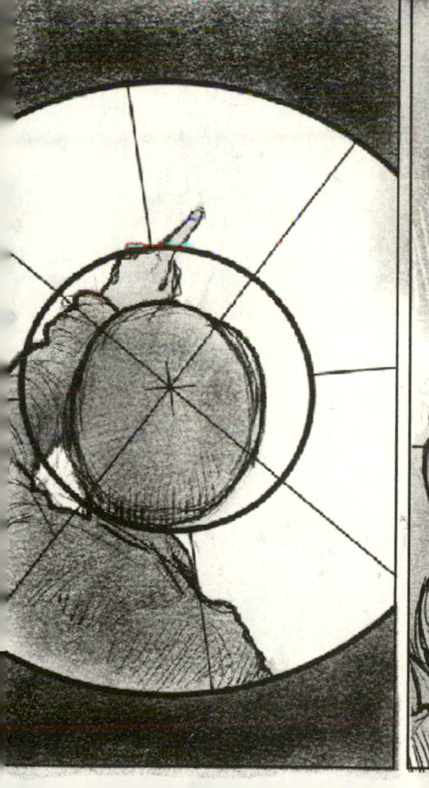

THAT'S AN OR...
ZING
THWACK!
GET DOWN, SIR!
...DER ...DER ...DER.

OH...
...CRUD.
OOF.
WUMP!

IS HE DEAD, MAK? IS HE DEAD?
HOW DO I KNOW?
HERE, HELP ME ROLL HIM OVER.
TAKE HIS HELMET OFF.
NOT ME! HIS BRAINS'LL FALL OUT.
NO THEY WON'T. THE BULLET JUST GRAZED HIS HELMET. LOOK, IT'S BARELY DENTED. C'MON, HARRY. GRAB HIS CANTEEN AND GIVE HIM SOME WATER.

HE'S IN THE CHURCH TOWER, VINCE!
YA, I GOT HIM.
WHAT HAPPENED? WHERE AM I? WHO ARE YOU?
HOLD HIS HEAD UP AND I'LL GIVE HIM A DRINK.

LATER...
ALL CLEAR UP HERE, CAP'N.

ALL RIGHT, BOYS. YOU'RE FREE TO MOVE AROUND.
BUT STAY SHARP!

HOW'S YOUR LIEUTENANT?
HE'S FINE, SIR.
MERRY CHRISTMAS.
HE DOESN'T SOUND FINE.

WAIT A SECOND. I JUST REMEMBERED SOMETHING. I WAS SHOT IN THE HEAD.
THE BULLET GRAZED YOUR HELMET AND YOU GOT STUNNED. THAT'S ALL.
BUT... BUT I'M BLEEDING!
THAT'S NOT BLOOD, SIR. THAT'S JUST WATER. YOU'RE GOING TO BE FINE.
FINE?
HOW DO YOU KNOW? YOU'RE NOT A MEDIC! YOU'RE JUST A MAK.
YOU'RE RIGHT, SIR. I'M NOT A MEDIC. BUT THERE'S HARDLY EVEN A DENT IN YOUR HEL--
I WANT A MEDIC RIGHT NOW!

HERE I AM, SIR.
OW.
OW.
OW.
LET ME TAKE A LOOK AT YOU.
BE CAREFUL, PRIVATE. I'VE BEEN SHOT IN THE HEAD.

WELL, FROM WHAT I CAN SEE...
...YOU AIN'T GOT NO HEAD WOUND.

WHAT ARE YOU TALKING ABOUT?!
LIKE I SAID, SIR. FROM WHAT I CAN SEE, YOU AIN'T BEEN SHOT IN THE HEAD.
BUT I REMEMBER BEING SHOT! RIGHT HERE! IN MY HEAD!
I'M SORRY TO DISAPPOINT YOU, SIR, BUT YOU AIN'T GOT NO HEAD WOUND. I SEEN PLENTY OF HEAD WOUNDS THESE PAST FEW DAYS AND BELIEVE ME, YOU AIN'T GOT ONE.

NOW...
...AS I TAKE A PEEK AT YER HELMET HERE, I CAN SEE IT GOT GRAZED BY A BULLET. AND THAT CAN FEEL LIKE THE OLD NOODLE BEEN WHACKED BY A HAMMER. BUT IT COULDA BEEN A LOT WORSE, SIR. LEMME TELL YA, YOU'RE ONE LUCKY SON OF A GUN.

LUCKY?! I WAS SHOT IN THE HEAD, YOU NINCOMPOOP!
YEP, VERY LUCKY.
HELMET, SIR. YOU GOT A DENT IN YOUR HELMET, NOT YOUR HEAD.
ALL RIGHT, I'VE HAD ENOUGH OF THIS! WHERE ARE YOU GOING WITH THAT AMBULANCE?

TO THE REAR, SIR. TO A FIELD HOSPITAL. WE'RE FULL UP WITH WOUNDED.
HELP ME UP. I'M COMING WITH YOU.
BUT WE AIN'T GOT NO ROOM, SIR.
UNLESS YOU RIDE UP FRONT WITH ME AND RODNEY. BUT WE'RE PRETTY TIGHT UP THERE ALREADY.
IS THIS WHAT THEY TEACH YOU IN MEDIC SCHOOL?! TO ARGUE WITH A WOUNDED OFFICER? HELP ME UP!
YOU GET ME TO A HOSPITAL RIGHT NOW! THAT'S AN ORDER.
YES, SIR.

SHOVE OVER, RODNEY. THIS LIEUTENANT IS GONNA HITCH A RIDE WITH US. HE THINKS HE'S GOT A HEAD INJURY.
I DON'T *THINK* I HAVE A HEAD INJURY, PRIVATE. I *HAVE* A HEAD INJURY!
OH, YES, SIR. SORRY, SIR.
MAK. WHAT JUST HAPPENED?
GOOD QUESTION.
DID WE JUST LOSE OUR LIEUTENANT?
UH, YEAH. I THINK WE DID.
WHAT ARE WE GONNA DO?
ANOTHER GOOD QUESTION.

EXCUSE ME, SIR.
BUT WHAT DO YOU WANT US TO DO NOW?

WELL, I THINK YOU SHOULD CARRY ON. EXECUTE YOUR MISSION.
OUR MISSION? DOES THAT MEAN YOU WANT US TO GO ON TO BRUYÈRES WITHOUT YOU?
THAT'S AN EXCELLENT IDEA, CORPORAL! GO TO BRUYÈRES!

Please be good for Mom and Pop. You are always in my heart.
Love, your big brother Mak

17. THAT "FEENO" SHOT

When I woke up, I noticed that my head felt like it was packed in big wads of cotton. I lay there for a moment, rolling my head back and forth and investigating this new sensation.

I tried to open my eyes but quickly squeezed them shut again. It was so bright, almost like I'd woken up inside a lightbulb. In the brief moment my eyes were open, I'd seen that I was in a large room, that I was in a bed surrounded by several empty beds. Sunlight was pouring in through the windows, and everything it touched seemed to be lit up from within—the white blankets, the walls, the floor. My eyes stung and tears began to flow. I tried to raise my hands to rub the sting and tears out of my eyes but found that I couldn't. I opened my eyes again and saw that someone had tied my wrists to the railing on either side of my bed with strips of cloth.

I heard someone crying nearby. More like whimpering than crying. Whoever it was seemed so close, they could've been in the same bed with me. I felt the bed start to bounce up and down. This frightened me. Maybe we were having an earthquake. I tried to free my arms. I pulled and pulled on the strips of cloth, but nothing came of it but an ache in my wrists.

The whimpering turned to crying. It sounded like a girl's voice. I wanted to help her. I wanted to tell her that we were going to be okay, it was just a little earthquake. She kept crying.

I heard footsteps. Someone was coming toward me. Maybe it was the girl. Maybe she'd untie my wrists and we could get out of the building. I felt hands on my shoulders. The bed stopped bouncing up and down. Thank goodness, the earthquake had stopped! I wanted to thank the girl for stopping the earthquake. I risked more stinging and tears and opened my eyes for a second. The person leaning over me wasn't a girl. It was a grown-up, a woman. She was dressed all in white. The way the sunlight fell upon her little hat made it look like the top of her head was on fire. I squeezed my eyes shut.

"Doctor! Doctor!"

More rushing footsteps. I opened my eyes again. The woman with her head on fire had been joined by another grown-up; this one was a man. He looked familiar. I decided not to try to figure out why.

"Her fever is back and she is grinding her teeth," said the woman.

"Let's give her another shot," said the man. "It's been several hours since the first."

The whimpering started again. I wished someone would help the girl.

"Yes," said the woman. "Here."

"Keep her from fidgeting."

I felt a small sting. My wrists stopped aching. The girl whimpered for a little while longer and then was silent.

"Can you get her parents?" I heard the man say. "I want to talk with them while she's out."

I don't remember falling asleep, but that's what must've happened, because I woke up and found Mama seated by me on the bed, holding my hand. Father stood nearby talking to the man.

"But she thinks she's a bird," said Father. "This is abnormal."

"She was just pretending, Ichiro," said Mama.

"I would like to hear what the doctor has to say, Aki," Father replied.

"Well," said the doctor, "she has been under tremendous stress these past few weeks. And to accompany that, she is still recovering from pneumonia. Behaving as she did last night, well, that might just be a way for Mari's mind to work through all that has happened to her."

"But you have a cure, right?" said Father. "That shot you gave her, that 'feeno' shot, that will cure her of whatever this is, right?"

"Well, no," said the doctor. "While phenobarbital is a wonderful medication, it is a stopgap measure at best. She was in such a state when you brought her in, and again this morning, that the shot was the most effective method for calming her."

"What do we do now, Doctor?" I heard Mama say.

"We must wait and allow Mari to rest. When her fever comes down and she regains a sense of calm, then she can go back to be with you in your barracks. Then she must have complete bed rest for two or three weeks, perhaps more. I'll give you some sleeping medication to mix in with her food at night. After that, we can talk again."

"But then she'll be cured?" said Father. "After that period of rest she'll be cured?"

"I really can't say, Mr. Asai," said the doctor. "I'm not sure that she needs to be 'cured' of anything. She just needs time and complete rest."

"May I stay with Mari until we can take her back to our barracks?" I heard Mama say.

"Yes," said the doctor. "That would be fine."

I heard footsteps moving away. I fell asleep again and awoke to find someone was stroking my forehead. I opened my eyes. Mama was still sitting beside me. Father and the doctor had moved across the room and were talking quietly. Mama put her hand on my cheek. Her hand was cool. It felt nice.

"Mama," I said, forgetting my vow again, "do you like cinnamon?"

"Yes. I do."

"Me too," I replied. "What happened to the girl?" I continued.

"What girl?"

"The one who was crying. Is she okay?"

"Oh, yes," said Mama. "Yes, she is fine now. Why don't you sleep for a bit?"

I thought for a moment, *I broke my vow again,* but quickly realized I didn't much care. With Mama beside me, holding my hand, I closed my eyes and fell asleep.

10/24/44
Dear Mari,
This is such a beautiful place. Maybe someday we could come back to visit.

HEY, THIS GUY LOOKS KINDA FRIENDLY. MAYBE HE KNOWS WHERE BRUYÈRES IS.
I'LL GO TALK TO HIM.
VENEZ VITE!

CONDUISEZ RAPIDEMENT ET NON EN LIGNE DROITE. COMPRENEZ?
D'ACCORD. MERCI. MERCI BEAUCOUP.

WHAT'D THE PARTISAN SAY?
BRUYÈRES IS JUST AROUND THE CORNER. SHOULDN'T TAKE MORE THAN A FEW MINUTES. BUT HE ALSO SAID THAT A KRAUT MORTAR CREW HAS SNUCK BACK BEHIND OUR LINES AND IS SHELLING THE ROAD.

WELL, WHAT DO YOU WANNA DO?
I WANNA GO HOME.
FUNNY. BUT SERIOUSLY, MAK, YOU OUTRANK ME. WHAT DO WE DO?
I GUESS WE GET IN THE JEEP, DRIVE LIKE CRAZY TO BRUYÈRES, AND HOPE WE DON'T GET BLOWN TO PIECES ON THE WAY THERE.
I DON'T KNOW WHY I ASK YOU QUESTIONS. YOU ALWAYS SAY STUFF I DON'T WANNA HEAR.

I MAY HAVE TO DO SOME CREATIVE DRIVING SO HOLD ON TIGHT.
WILL DO.
YOU OKAY?
NOPE.
OKAY. HERE WE GO.

DO YOU GOTTA DRIVE THIS FAST?
IF YOU DON'T WANT US TO GET BLOWN UP I DO.

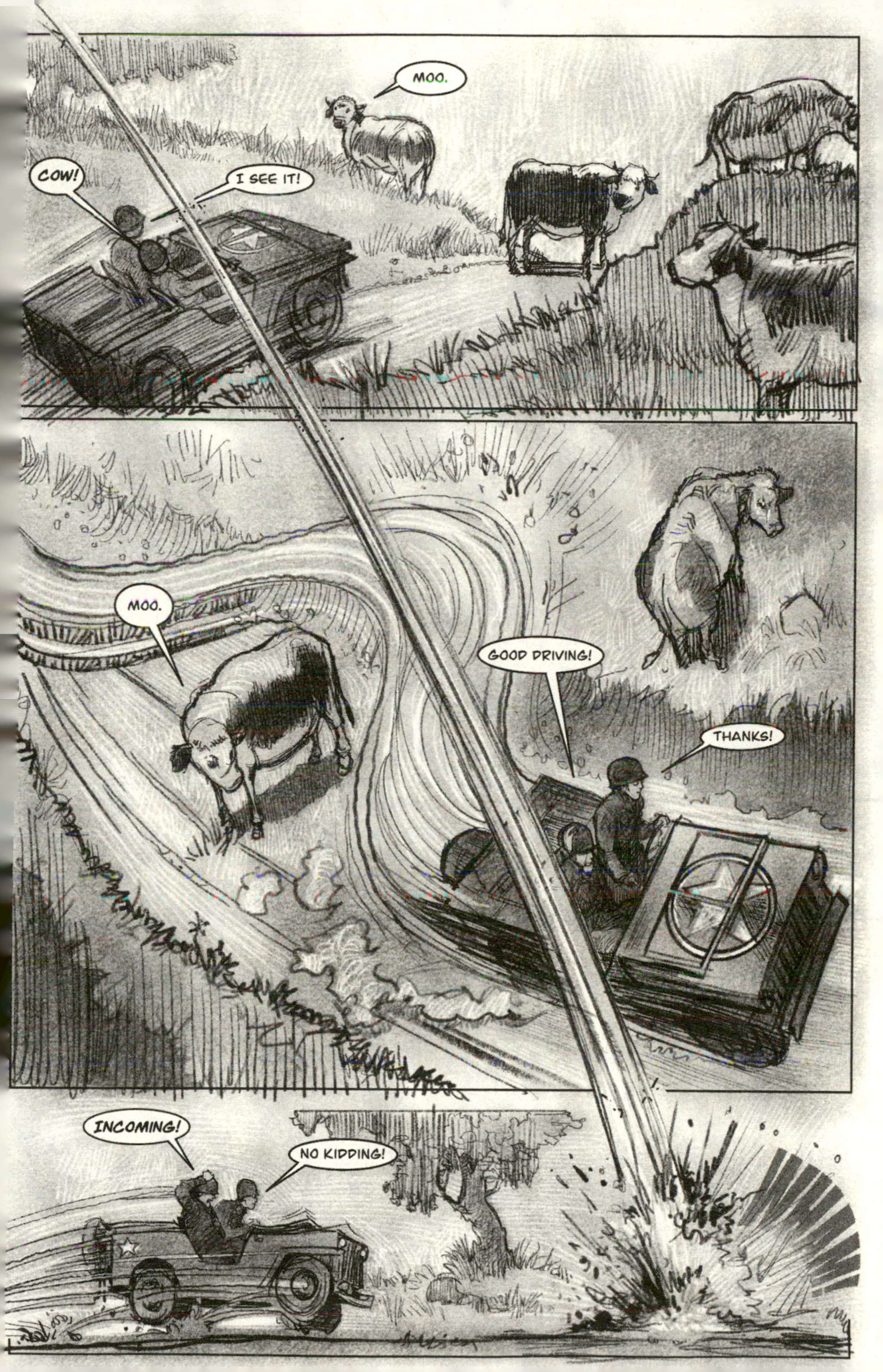
MOO.
COW!
I SEE IT!
MOO.
GOOD DRIVING!
THANKS!
INCOMING!
NO KIDDING!

HARRY!
YOU ALL RIGHT OVER THERE, SOLDIER?
UH, YES, SIR.
GOOD.
YOU MAY COMMENCE FIRING, SERGEANT.
YES, SIR.

FIRE!
BLAM!

BLAM!
KEEP UP THAT RATE OF FIRE, SERGEANT.
YOU BOYS SEE WHERE THEM KRAUT MORTAR ROUNDS WERE COMING FROM?
NO, SIR. SORRY, SIR.
DON'T MATTER NONE. WE'LL GET THE WEASEL.
WUMP!
WUMP!
YOU BOYS NEED ANYTHING?
YES, SIR. HOW FAR IS BRUYÈRES FROM HERE?
WUMP!
HOW FAR? HECK, BOY, YOU'RE SITTIN' IN THE BRUYÈRES VILLAGE SCHOOLYARD.
WUMP!
WUMP!
AND THE COMMAND POST, SIR?
COMMAND POST IS IN THE TOWN HALL. JUST UP THE HILL ON YOUR LEFT. CAN'T MISS IT.

LET'S GET OUT OF HERE.
YOU OKAY TO WALK?
WHAT?
HOW ARE YOUR EARS DOING?
HUH?
I SAID...

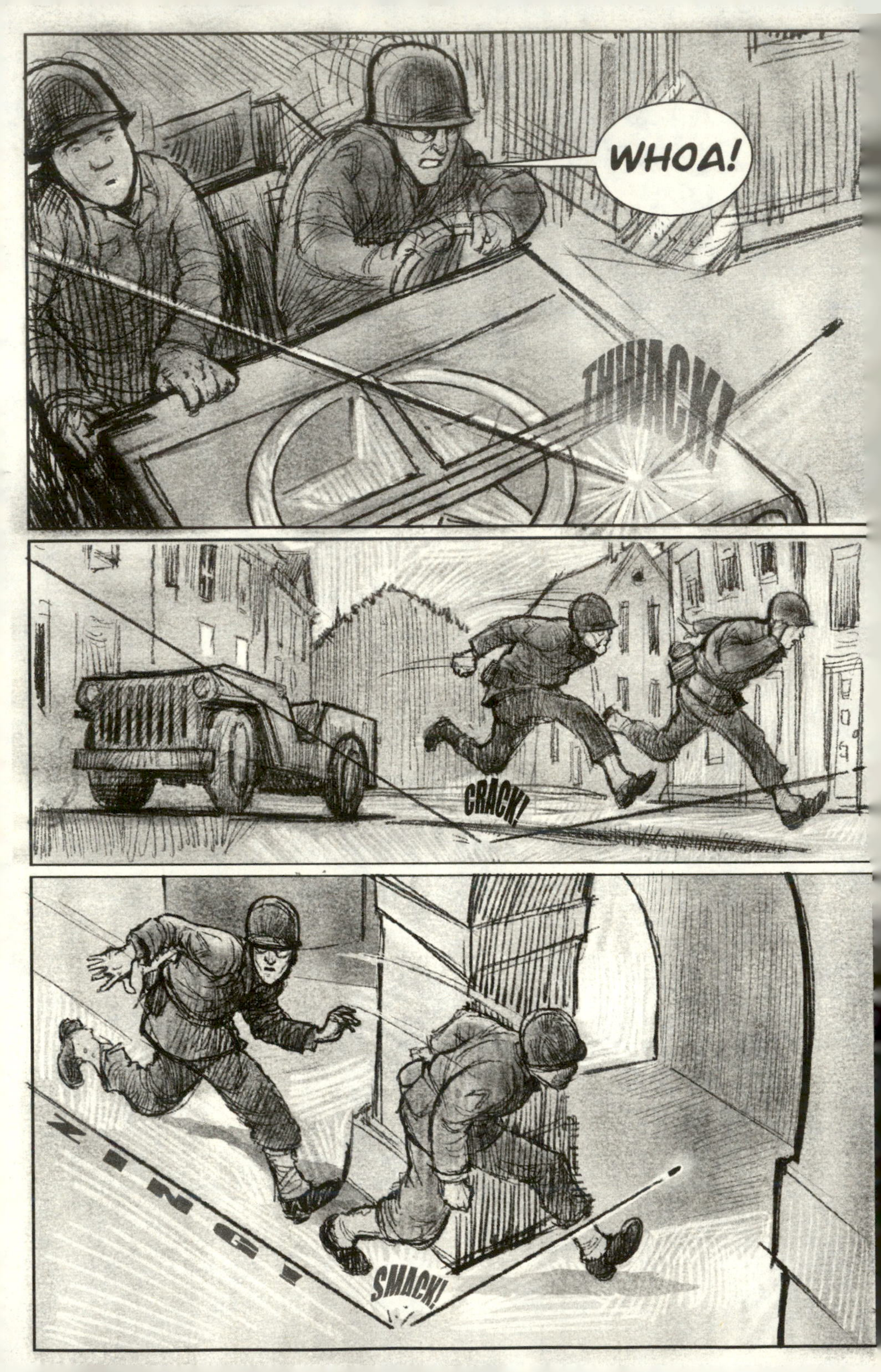
WHOA!
THWACK!
CRACK!
ZING!
SMACK!

WELCOME TO BRUYÈRES. FIRST TIME IN A COMBAT ZONE?
Y-YEAH.
YOU'RE REPLACEMENTS, RIGHT?
UH... Y-YES.
YOU WON AGAIN, JIMMY! HERE Y'GO.
HA! I TOLD YOU THEY WAS REPLACEMENTS!
I CAN SPOT A REPLACEMENT FROM A MILE AWAY.
SO, WHAT BRINGS YOU BOYS TO THE FRONT LINE?
WE'RE L-LOOKING FOR THE C-COMMAND POST.
WELL, YOU'RE IN LUCK, BRUDDAH.
THE COLONEL IS RIGHT DOWN THE BOTTOM OF THESE STAIRS.
TH-THANKS.

C'MON, HARRY, LET'S GO.
WHAT?
JUST GO!
AND LISTEN, YOU'RE GOING TO WANNA RIP THEM RANK STRIPES OFF YOUR ARM. THE KRAUTS LIKE TO USE 'EM FOR TARGET PRACTICE.
SAY HI TO THE COLONEL FOR US!
AND DON'T FORGET TO ASK HIM FOR A SPECIAL ASSIGNMENT.
HEH, HEH. THE COLONEL JUST LOVES HANDING OUT THEM SPECIAL ASSIGNMENTS.

DOWNSTAIRS
EXCUSE ME, COLONEL, SIR.
MAKE IT FAST, CORPORAL. I'M BUSY.
YES, SIR. REGIMENTAL COMMAND WOULD LIKE A STATUS REPORT.
THE GENERAL SENT YOU TO CHECK UP ON US, DID HE?
WELL, NOT ME, SIR. OUR LIEUTENANT. BUT THE THING IS HE GOT SHOT IN THE... HELMET A FEW MILES BACK AND SENT US ON AHEAD, SIR.
SHOT IN THE HELMET, HUH? SOUNDS FASCINATING.
Y'SEE, NATE?! THIS IS EXACTLY WHAT I WAS TALKING ABOUT! THE POMPOUS TWIT GIVES US AN IMPOSSIBLE ORDER, AND THEN HE'S GOTTA KEEP STICKIN' HIS NOSE IN IT ALL DAY LONG!
CAREFUL, SIR. YOU'RE STARTING TO SOUND A LITTLE MUTINOUS.
CAREFUL?! HA! WHAT DO I KNOW ABOUT BEING CAREFUL?

I WANT YOU TO TAKE A LOOK AROUND AND TELL ME WHAT YOU SEE HANGING ON THE WALLS.
UH, PHONE LINES, SIR?
THAT'S RIGHT. AND ARE SOLDIERS TALKING ON THE PHONES?
YES, SIR.
THAT MEANS YOUR MISSION HAS BECOME REDUNDANT.
SIR?
WE SPLICED THE PHONE LINES TOGETHER THIS MORNING AND BEEN TALKING TO THE GENERAL SINCE LUNCH. YOU'RE OUT OF A JOB, SON.
OH.

NOTHING SADDER THAN A SOLDIER WITHOUT A MISSION. BUT DON'T WORRY. I'VE GOT A SPECIAL ASSIGNMENT FOR YOU.
THANK YOU, SIR.
DON'T THANK ME, SON. I CAN ASSURE YOU THERE IS NOTHING ABOUT THIS ASSIGNMENT THAT'S WORTH YOUR GRATITUDE.
SERGEANT KURODA, FRONT AND CENTER!
SERGEANT, DO YOU RECALL THAT PLAN WE TALKED ABOUT THAT INVOLVED USING JEEPS TO RETRIEVE THE WOUNDED?
YES, SIR. I DO.
GOOD. GET THIS CORPORAL'S JEEP RIGGED FOR THAT DUTY AND EXPLAIN HIS NEW MISSION TO HIM.
CAN DO, SIR.
WHEN WE GET UP TO THE TOP OF THE STAIRS WE'LL TAKE A SEAT AND I'LL FILL YOU IN ON YOUR NEW ASSIGNMENT. UNDERSTOOD?
YES, SERGEANT.

ALL RIGHT, LISTEN UP. THE FRONT LINE IS UP IN THE HILLS ABOUT A MILE FROM HERE.
THERE'S NO ROADS TO SPEAK OF UP THERE. AMBULANCES CAN'T GET TO THE WOUNDED. ONLY THING THAT CAN GET UP THERE IS A JEEP. SINCE YOU BOY'S JUST SUPPLIED THE COLONEL WITH YOUR NICE NEW JEEP, YOU BEEN PROMOTED. YOU'RE NOW JEEP-AMBULANCE DRIVERS.
AMBULANCE DRIVERS?! HOLD ON A SECOND! I'M NOT A MEDIC!
YOU DON'T GOTTA FIX THE WOUNDED, MAC. YOU JUST GOTTA GET 'EM AND BRING 'EM BACK.
WAIT. HOW DID YOU KNOW MY NAME IS MAK?
I DIDN'T.

I CALL ALL YOU NEW GUYS MAC. MOST OF YOU END UP WOUNDED OR DEAD BEFORE I LEARN YOUR NAME ANYWAY. SO TO ME YOU'RE ALL JUST MAC.
NOW PAY ATTENTION--OUT IN THE SQUARE, YOU BETTER RUN TO THAT JEEP LIKE YOUR PANTS ARE ON FIRE. DON'T RUN IN A STRAIGHT LINE AND DON'T CLIMB MY TAIL. SNIPERS LOVE PLUGGING TWO GI'S WITH THE SAME SLUG.
WHEN WE GET TO THE JEEP, I'LL DO THE DRIVING. WE'LL GRAB SOME CHOW WHILE A MECHANIC RIGS THE JEEP FOR STRETCHER DUTY.
THEN YOU TWO DRIVE UP TO THE FRONT, GET THE WOUNDED, AND BRING 'EM BACK TO THE AID STATION.
PIECE OF CAKE.
UNDERSTOOD?

I, UH... YEAH, I UNDERSTAND. BUT HOW'RE WE--
GOOD.
WHEN I SAY "GO" WE RUN FOR THE JEEP.
GOT IT, MAC?
UH, MAK.
SURE, BUT--
GO!

MAK?!
RUN, HARRY!

I know you must hear about terrible battles, but I don't want you to worry about me. The war is almost over, and I will be home soon! Love, your big brother Mak

18. JUST ME

The doctor let me go home the next day. He didn't want Father to carry me, but he didn't want me to walk back to our barracks either. So he suggested that I ride back to the barracks in one of the camp's fire trucks. He was just trying to be nice, and I guess he thought it might be a treat for me, but it wasn't. Even though I still wasn't feeling very good, I would much rather have just walked. I didn't want to make a big fuss about going back to our barracks by riding in a fire truck. And I especially didn't want them to turn on the truck's siren. I had to fight with the driver all the way back to keep him from turning on the stupid thing. He was very disappointed with me. That's okay. I wasn't too happy with him, either.

I slept a lot over the next few days. I mean *a lot* a lot. I slept next to Mama so she could keep an eye on me, and Father moved into my bed. Mama'd wake me up to eat some soup or use the bedpan, and then I'd go right back to sleep. It took a while, but I did start to feel better.

Even so, we spent a lot of time in our barracks after that. You can't imagine what it's like to be stuck with your parents for days on end in a space that's twenty feet by twenty feet. I nearly went crazy.

Sometimes it was okay, though. For instance, Father brought books from the camp library, and Mama and I would read them out loud. Since they were all in English, I did most of the reading. I liked one of the books very much—*Lost Horizon*. The story is about this group of people who get lost in the mountains in Tibet and are saved by these priests—called lamas—who bring them back to their monastery. The place is so magical that it keeps people feeling young and happy no matter what their age. Sort of like Manzanar, only the exact opposite.

Father also brought our meals from the mess hall, and we'd eat together at our little table. After we ate dessert, I'd get very tired, which was odd because I wasn't getting any exercise. I didn't understand why until one night, when Mama and I were about to eat our evening dish of applesauce, I saw Father crush a pill and put it into my serving. I thought that pill must be what made me so sleepy. I didn't mind knowing that. Because for a while, at least, I was scared to go to sleep at night. I never wanted to wake up and find I'd become a bird, or anything else, ever again.

There were a lot of holes in my memory of that night and the day in the hospital. Mama filled me in on a lot of what had happened: my wearing bits of camouflage and pretending to be a bird, who the girl was who'd been crying. (Hint—it was me.) Mama told me that we hadn't had any earthquakes. I was surprised by this. She guessed that my fever and the drug they gave me had unsettled me to the point where I started thrashing about and bouncing in the bed. I had been so out of it that I couldn't tell the difference between my having a fit and the camp having an earthquake. I don't like being sick.

While there was so much that I couldn't remember, there was one thing I really couldn't forget—the cinnamon dream. I've had lots of dreams, but that one was so odd. And it seemed so real. I kept seeing it in my imagination for days afterward—Oba-chan Yuki bear sitting on the big purple heart medal, and little red puppy Keiko laughing and waving her wooden spoon, her face covered in cinnamon dust. One night I even dreamed of Mak and his sausage fingers again. This time not only was the guitar orange with purple polka dots, but so was Mak. He was playing that little guitar thing, and he sounded pretty good. When he'd finished his song, he looked at me and said, "Go for Broke, kabocha-head." It was so weird, and I didn't know what any of that meant, but I liked seeing all of them.

I woke right after that dream. It was still dark. I sat looking at Mak's picture on the table next to the bed. I wanted so much just to talk with him. The picture was one of those formal high school pictures where people always try to look so serious. But no matter how serious he might try to be, he was still goofy Mak to me, with those silly glasses and his tilted smile. I cried for a little while, looking at him. Then I got up and walked over to the table where my drawing pad was.

Some kids like to draw stuff from their imagination. Not me. I like to draw real things—birds, flowers, mountains, and even Eunice's skulls. But this morning I just had to get these images from my dream onto a piece of paper. So I did.

Page after page. I don't know how long I sat there drawing, but the sun had risen when I heard Father make one of his before-breakfast-coffee groans.

"Mari. That's . . . that is a lot of drawings."

I looked at Father and smiled. Then I looked at the wall where I had stuck my drawings. We didn't have any sticky tape, so I'd used little pieces of clay. Mama had bought the clay for me when I thought I might become a famous sculptor. I had put little pieces in the corners of each drawing and just stuck them up wherever there was empty wall space. There must've been twenty or thirty pieces of paper up there.

It was an impressive sight. Even a little scary because I didn't remember making some of the drawings. Also, some were a little weird. I stretched puppy Keiko's wooden spoon in one drawing, so it looked like she was swinging a tennis racket; in another I'd shown Oba-chan bear riding the purple heart medal like it was a motorboat cutting through waves of cinnamon dust. Just a little weird. But fun! And they were good. Eunice would say they had "good bones." Father came to stand beside me. He rubbed his stubbly chin, considering my morning's work.

"Did you do all of these just now? You haven't been up all night, have you?"

Mama was up. She came to stand by Father.

"Oh my, Mari," she said. "You have been busy."

I smiled, then looked down at the drawing I'd been

working on. Mak was looking up at me from the paper, his smiling face, body, and the guitar thing covered in polka dots. I'd drawn the polka dots sliding off of Mak, flowing about the page and transforming into musical notes. I also drew a word balloon, like in the comics, next to Mak's face. In it I wrote, *Go for Broke, kabocha-head!* Father looked over my shoulder.

"Hey, look at this! This is a wonderful drawing of your brother. But . . . you . . . you've given him the mumps. Look at all the dots on him."

I looked at Father and squinched my nose at him. *Mumps? Those aren't mumps! They're polka dots!*

"Oh, Mari," said Mama. "Such a lovely drawing of Mak. And look at this little guitar he is playing."

I nodded and smiled, trying to forget Father's mumps remark.

"Oh yes," said Father, "I see. You've drawn Mak holding a ukulele. One of the men in barracks twenty-six has one. I heard him play it once. Oh yes, this is a ukulele."

Again more nodding, more smiling.

"Well," said Father. "It looks quite nice outside. Perhaps we could all go to breakfast. What do you think, Aki?"

"I think that is a very good idea," said Mama.

I felt so happy, I didn't know what to do. So I stood up and gave Father a hug. He stood there just as he always did when I hugged him, his arms slightly away from his sides and a look of surprise on his face, as if I were giving him the first hug he'd ever gotten. I looked up at him. He was smiling down at me. It was a warm, gentle smile, the kind that I didn't often see on his face. Tears popped out of the corners of my eyes. I hugged him harder, pressed my head tight against his belly. I could feel his heartbeat. I wanted to hold him like that and keep that smile on his face forever.

Father chuckled nervously. "Hey now," he said, awkwardly patting the top of my head. "Hey."

I kept hugging him, afraid to let him go. Afraid that that rare smile would be replaced with the face Father usually showed to me. He patted me lightly on the back.

"Come now, Mari," said Father. "Time for breakfast."

I let him go, trying not to look at him. I wanted to keep that picture of his smiling face in my mind for as long as I could. I might need it again someday.

We got dressed and headed for the door. I thought of how I might draw that smile and grabbed my sketchbook. I could see it clearly in my mind's eye. I most definitely needed to draw this smile. As we walked to the mess hall, I started to feel a strange sensation. I felt lighter, sort of bouncy, and the air smelled good, almost yummy. *What is this?* I thought. Mama looked down at me and smiled. I smiled back.

"It is good to see you happy again, Mari," she said.

Oh, I thought, *so that's what this feeling is. I'm happy.*

10/25/44

Dear Mari,

Just a quick note to say that I am well. I hope you are too. Please hug Mom and Pop for me. And give yourself a hug too.

Love, your big brother Mak

HOW'RE YOUR EARS?
BETTER. THEY'RE STILL RINGING, BUT AT LEAST I CAN HEAR NOW.
GOOD. C'MON, LET'S GO IN.

I'M GETTING THAT LOST FEELING AGAIN. WE'RE NOT LOST, ARE WE, MAK?
NO, HARRY, WE'RE NOT LOST. OKAY?
I TOLD YOU TWICE ALREADY-- THE SERGEANT SAID WE SHOULD GO TO THE FIELD HOSPITAL IN THE CHURCH TO GET DIRECTIONS.
OH, MAN.

WHO DO WE ASK FOR DIRECTIONS?
YOUR GUESS IS AS GOOD AS MINE. YOU TAKE THAT SIDE AND I'LL TAKE THIS.

EXCUSE ME, COULD YOU GIVE ME DIRECTIONS TO THE FRONT LINE?
NOPE.
SAY, PAL, CAN YOU, UH, POINT ME TO THE FRONT LINES?
NO.
EXCUSE ME, DOCTOR, UH, SIR, CAN YOU DIRECT US TO THE FRONT LINE? WE'RE--
I'M GOING TO STOP YOU RIGHT THERE, CORPORAL.
IN CASE YOU HADN'T NOTICED, THIS IS A VERY BUSY FIELD HOSPITAL. WE HAVE NO MAPS. NO COORDINATES. IN SHORT, WE CAN'T HELP YOU.
BUT, SIR, ALL WE--
THAT'S THE END OF THIS DISCUSSION, SOLDIER.
HERE'S MY RECOMMENDATION--GO BACK OUTSIDE, LISTEN FOR THE SOUND OF GUN FIRE, AND HEAD TOWARD IT. I HAVE NO DOUBT YOU'LL FIND THE FRONT LINE IN NO TIME AT ALL.
YOU'RE DISMISSED.

WHAT D'YA THINK, MAK? IS THIS ANY WAY TO RUN AN ARMY?
LIKE I SAID BEFORE-- CRAZY.
SO, WHAT DO WE DO NOW?
LET'S JUST GO OUTSIDE. SOMEBODY HAS GOT TO KNOW WHERE THE FRONT LINE IS. MAYBE AN AMBULANCE DRIVER WILL BE WILLING TO HELP US.

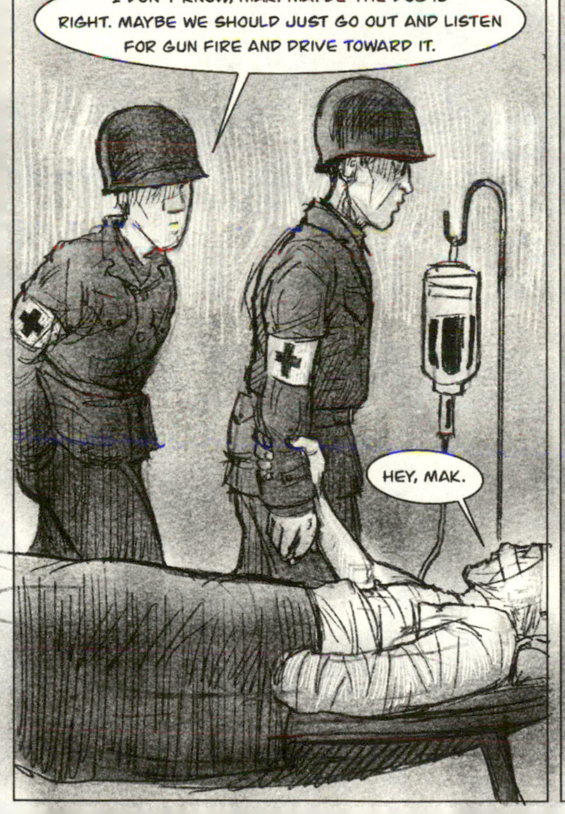
I DON'T KNOW, MAK. MAYBE THE DOC IS RIGHT. MAYBE WE SHOULD JUST GO OUT AND LISTEN FOR GUN FIRE AND DRIVE TOWARD IT.
HEY, MAK.

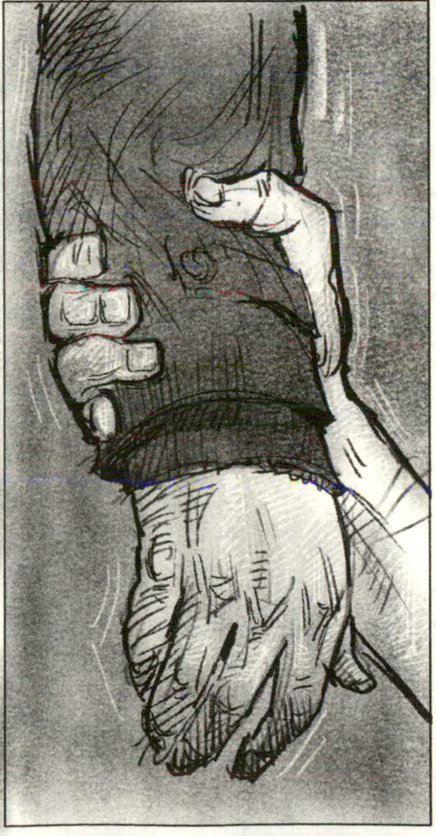

HUH?!
HEY, C'MON, LET GO.
HEY, BRUDDAH. HOW'S IT?

MAK. IT'S ME, YOUR OL' PAL KAZ.
SURPRISING
WHAT A LITTLE WAR CAN DO TO A GUY,
AIN'T IT?
K-KAZ?

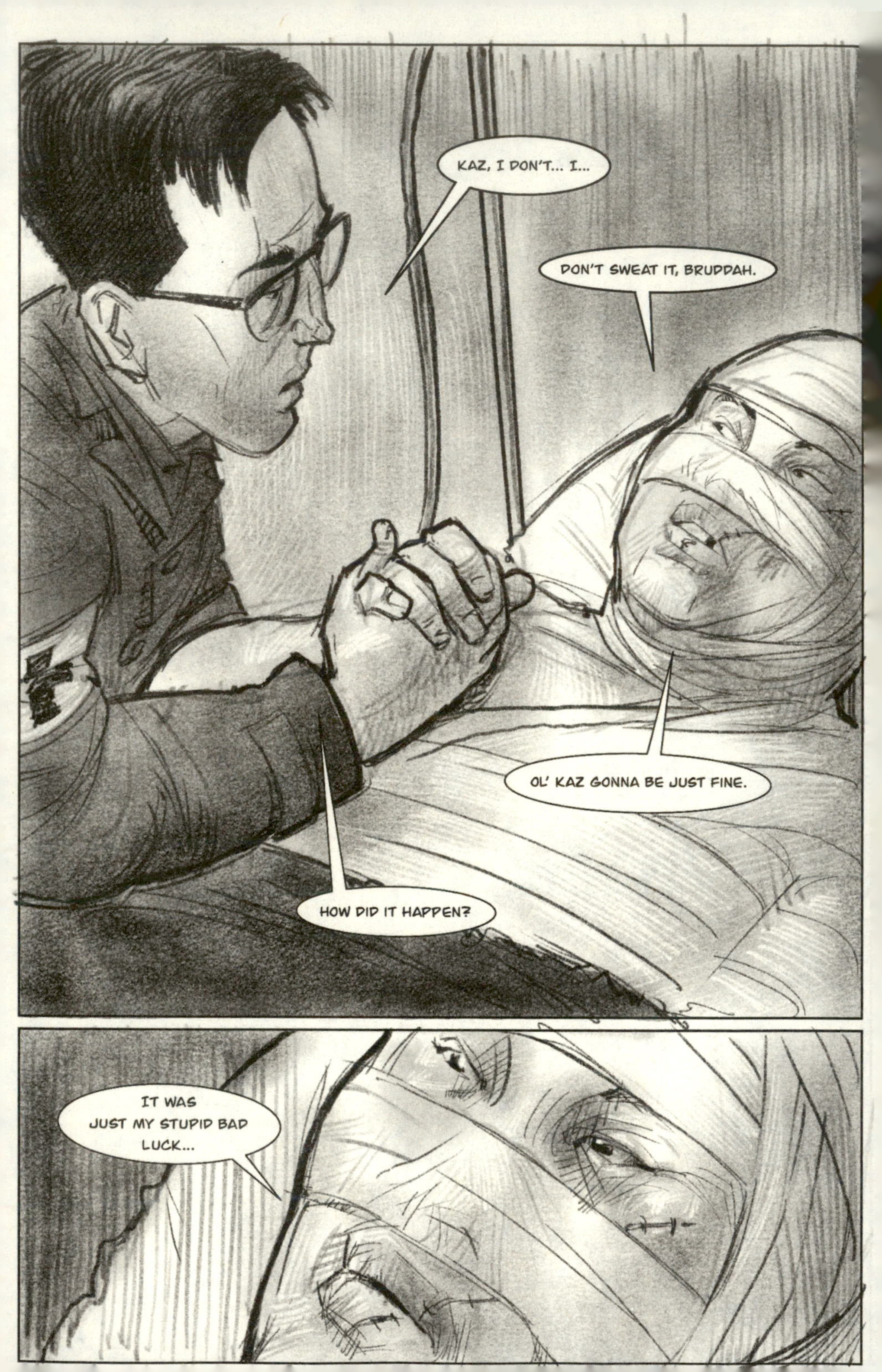
KAZ, I DON'T... I...
DON'T SWEAT IT, BRUDDAH.
OL' KAZ GONNA BE JUST FINE.
HOW DID IT HAPPEN?
IT WAS JUST MY STUPID BAD LUCK...

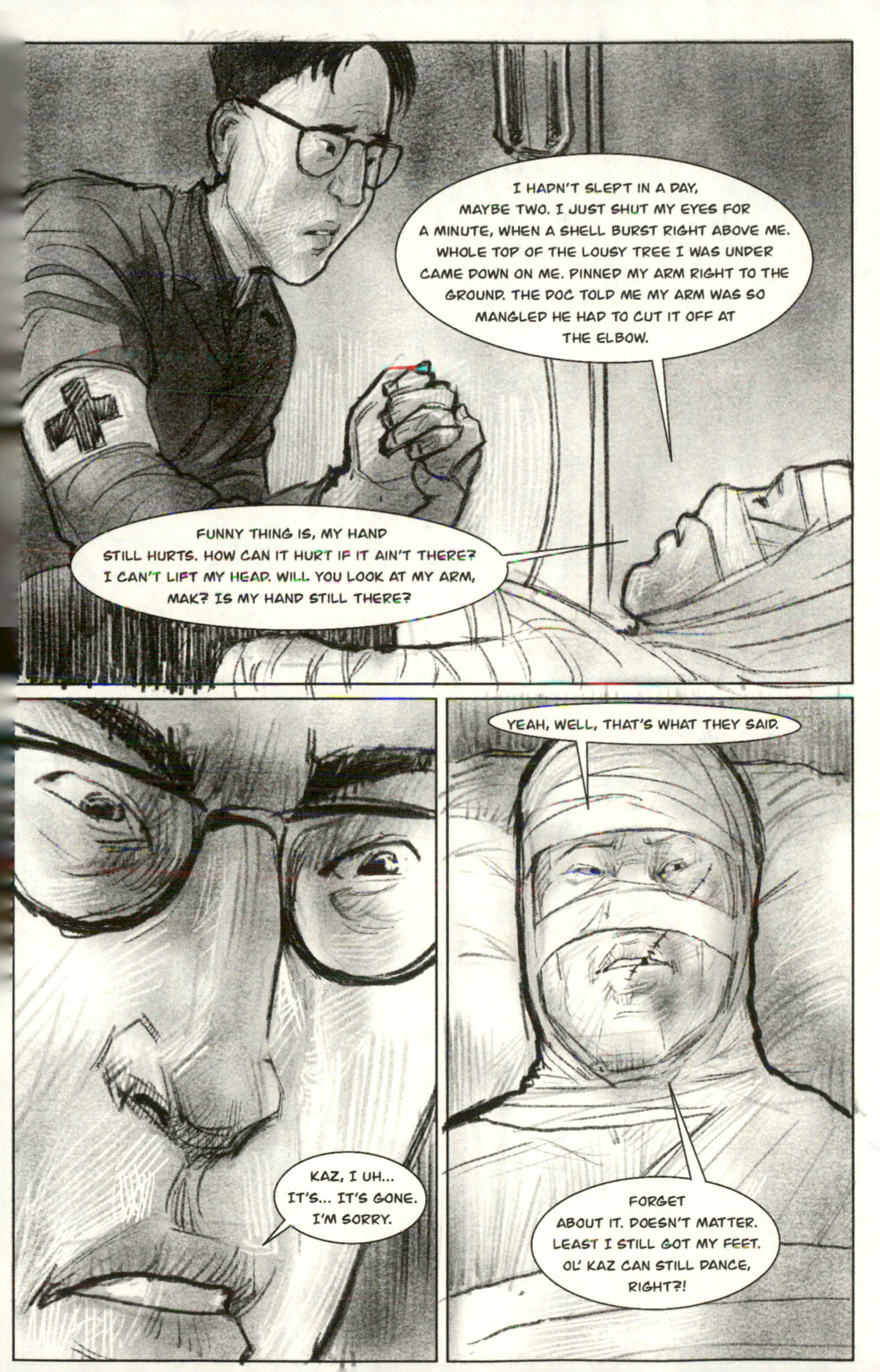
I HADN'T SLEPT IN A DAY, MAYBE TWO. I JUST SHUT MY EYES FOR A MINUTE, WHEN A SHELL BURST RIGHT ABOVE ME. WHOLE TOP OF THE LOUSY TREE I WAS UNDER CAME DOWN ON ME. PINNED MY ARM RIGHT TO THE GROUND. THE DOC TOLD ME MY ARM WAS SO MANGLED HE HAD TO CUT IT OFF AT THE ELBOW.
FUNNY THING IS, MY HAND STILL HURTS. HOW CAN IT HURT IF IT AIN'T THERE? I CAN'T LIFT MY HEAD. WILL YOU LOOK AT MY ARM, MAK? IS MY HAND STILL THERE?
KAZ, I UH... IT'S... IT'S GONE. I'M SORRY.
YEAH, WELL, THAT'S WHAT THEY SAID.
FORGET ABOUT IT. DOESN'T MATTER. LEAST I STILL GOT MY FEET. OL' KAZ CAN STILL DANCE, RIGHT?!

BUT
I GOTTA TELL YA,
MAK. IT'S GOOD TO
SEE YA.
IT'S
GOOD TO SEE YOU TOO,
KAZ.
SORRY, FELLAS.
VISITING HOURS ARE OVER. TIME TO CHANGE HIS
DRESSINGS.
OH. YEAH,
SURE.
MAK. WAIT.

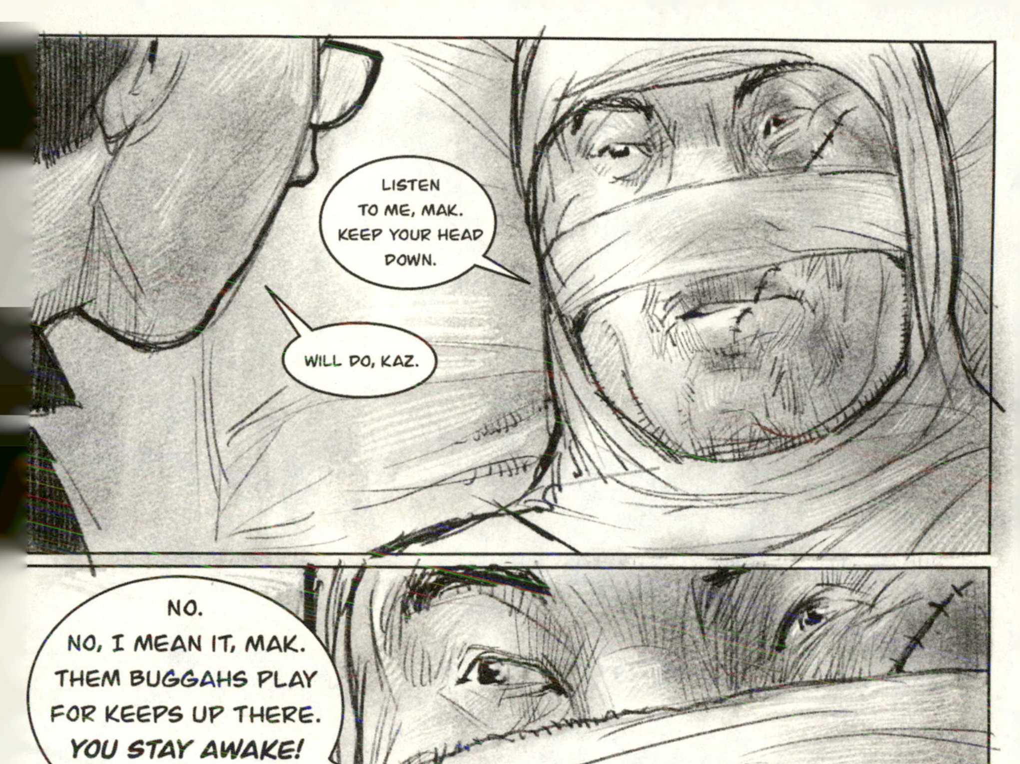
LISTEN TO ME, MAK. KEEP YOUR HEAD DOWN.
WILL DO, KAZ.
NO.
NO, I MEAN IT, MAK. THEM BUGGAHS PLAY FOR KEEPS UP THERE. *YOU STAY AWAKE!* YOU HEAR ME?

I HEAR YOU.
C'MON, MAK.
A HUI HOU, BRUDDAH.
GOODBYE, KAZ.

I'M SORRY ABOUT KAZ, MAK. HE'S A GOOD GUY.
YEAH, GOOD OL' KAZ. REAL GOOD ON THE UKULELE. FUNNY, TOO.
BUT, BOY, LOOK AT HIM NOW.
LISTEN, MAK, I WAS THINKING. IT DON'T SEEM LIKE SUCH A SMART IDEA FOR US TO DRIVE AROUND LOOKIN' FOR THE FRONT LINE IN THE MIDDLE OF THE NIGHT.

WHAT D'YA SAY WE SACK OUT RIGHT HERE AND HEAD OUT AT DAWN?
SURE. WHATEVER YOU SAY, HARRY.
WHY DON'T YOU GO AHEAD AND HOP UP ON THAT STRETCHER, AND I'LL PUT ONE OF THESE BLANKETS OVER YA.
OKAY.

THERE YA GO, MAK.
THANKS, HARRY.
I'LL BE BETTER IN THE MORNING.
YES, YOU WILL.

19. WAR IS EXPENSIVE

I rose early again and started drawing right away. It's amazing how much drawing you can get done in a day if you start before breakfast. Father peered at one of the drawings.

"You keep covering Mak in polka dots. Do you think he will like that?" he said.

Like it?! I thought angrily, *Of course he'll like it! Unlike some people in my family, Mak likes all my drawings!*

Mama must've noticed my angry eyebrows and squinched-up nose. She stepped between Father and me as she headed for the door.

"I am hungry!" she said while wrapping a kerchief over her hair. "Let's go have some breakfast."

The mess hall was quiet that morning. So many had left the camp using the government travel waiver program, going east as far as possible, that we didn't have to wait in line for breakfast. That was a nice change, but it was also a little sad, to still be there when so many had gone. After we'd eaten, I wrote a question to Mama on the back of one of my drawings. It said, *Can we go to the camouflage factory?*

"The camouflage factory? Are you sure about that?"

I nodded vigorously.

"Well," said Mama, "all right. But why?"

I held my sketchbook up in front of my face and shook it back and forth.

"For drawing? Hmmm . . . okay. Let's go, then. But we won't stay too long. I have some things for us to do before lunch."

We walked hand in hand across the camp. As we passed the school, I noticed how few kids there were on the playground. Maybe only a dozen. Two of them were boys from my class. They were brothers. One was chasing the other. The boy in front stopped abruptly when he saw me, and his brother ran right into him. They fell down in a pile. The whole thing looked like a scene from one of those silly silent movies where everybody is constantly running into one another. I would've laughed, but one of the boys was crying. I think they might've bumped their heads. The other stood up and waved at me.

"We're leaving soon," he called. "We're going to St. Louis."

He stood there staring at Mama and me as we walked away. His brother had gotten to his feet and was yelling at him, but he just kept staring at us. I don't know why he was looking at us that way. It's not like we had been friends. As Mama and I were about to turn a corner, I glanced back. He was still standing there, watching us. I raised my hand and waved. He jumped.

"G'bye!" he shouted.

I think his name was Sydney. I wanted to run back. Shake his hand. Tell him I knew St. Louis was far away, somewhere east of Manzanar, but that maybe we'd move to St. Louis too and we would be friends. *I'm going to run back,* I thought. *I'll run back and shake his hand.* But just then Mama came to a stop. I looked up. A slight breeze was blowing. The gray rags that hung from the rafters swayed to and fro, beckoning.

"Well, here we are," said Mama. "The camouflage factory."

We walked into the cavernous space. There were hardly any swallows today. But the wind was blowing, and little dust devils danced in and out of the sunlight. I was tempted to stick out my tongue and test for cinnamon. But I didn't. It'd take more than one weird dream to entice me to test whether the dust in Manzanar tasted like anything but dirt.

Besides, I hadn't come here for that. It was midmorning now, and the sunlight flowed at an angle through the factory. The rags continued to billow and flap, crissing and crossing the sun's rays, their shadows creating swirling patterns on the floor. I gazed at those patterns. That's what I'd come for.

I sat down on a log, Mama nearby. She had brought our thermos and two small cups. I opened my sketchbook and considered the blank sheet of paper, its brightness a challenge and an invitation. Mama placed a cup of tea on the ground by my foot. The rags flapped their lazy, crazy dance, and I took in their playful language as they wrote it for me on the floor in shadow and light. I'd brought charcoal to draw with. Without thinking, I began to mimic the movement of the shadows on the floor with the strokes of my hand on the paper.

"Come, dear," said Mama, placing her hand on my shoulder. "It's time to go."

I shied away from her, at first startled, then irritated. *I've just started drawing! How can you stop me when I've just started?* I considered saying something, breaking my silence. I was that angry. But then I looked down at my feet. All about where I sat were perhaps ten or twelve sheets of paper. One sheet after the other covered in complex patterns, knots, swirls, and waves of varying shades of gray and black. This, too, startled me. I didn't remember making all those drawings. I started to cry.

Mama moved closer. I leaned against her. It felt good to press my forehead against her shoulder. I cried for quite some time. First I cried for Mak and me. Then I cried for Mama and Father. And then for Oba-chan, Keiko, and even Sydney.

At last, when I was all cried out, Mama squeezed my hand, and we picked up my drawings, careful not to smudge them as we placed them in the pad. We walked back into camp, doing little chores along the way: picking up a package for Father in the mail room, visiting the doctor so he could take one last look at the small scar on my forehead. We ate lunch and went back to our barracks.

That afternoon we ambled about the camp. No reason why and no place to go. Just walking. Eventually our feet brought us to a Momoyama garden. This was the garden where the archway had stood that I had drawn. But the archway was gone. And so, it appeared, were the people who had made the garden. Tumbleweeds sat tangled in the bushes. Weeds were taking over where flowers had grown. It was just too sad. So we kept walking and, in time, found ourselves back at the mess hall. Again, no lines for supper. Just us, a few families, and a few single men in the big hall.

We ate lightly and made our way back to the barracks, the shadow of the Sierras following us all the way home while the sun set quickly behind them. We sat in bed and Mama read to me for a while. I soon fell into an uncomfortable sleep. I was so tired, but my mind kept racing, weaving weird little dreams, none of which I remembered when I swam up out of them.

Father came back late from a community meeting. Mama had been sitting up, waiting for him. I woke but stayed facing the wall, pretending to be asleep. This wasn't easy because I'd finally fallen into a real sleep and I was tired. But I wanted to hear what Father had to say.

"The camp administration believes that the exclusion order may be rescinded soon," he said.

"What does that mean to us, Ichiro?"

I could hear Father pacing back and forth.

"Well, one thing is we may be able to go back," said Father.

"Go back? Back where?" asked Mama.

"To our town."

"I do not want to go back there," whispered Mama.

"Florin is our home, Aki," replied Father.

"Not to me," said Mama. "I have not forgotten how they treated us."

Father sighed. I heard a chair being dragged away from

the table and the creak it made as Father sat down. Mama had warmed the teapot on the barracks' heater. I heard water being poured and the tinkle of a little spoon as it was stirred inside a little cup.

"War is expensive," Father said. "The expense to keep us here no longer matches their fear of us. Closing this place will help them balance the books."

"I am sorry. This is just too much to think about right now," said Mama. "Let's get some sleep and we'll talk again tomorrow."

"Yes. Good night, Aki."

"Good night, Ichiro."

Mama climbed into bed with me. As I lay there next to her, I wondered how much a war cost and what size piggy bank you'd need to hold all that money. I imagined President Roosevelt riding on top of a mammoth piggy bank, grabbing at enormous coins as they fell from storm clouds above. It was an exciting image and I very much wanted to get up and draw it, but I was just too, too tired. Instead I said a prayer for Mak and fell fast asleep.

Western Union Telegram
10/26/44
To: MR. ICHIRO ASAI
MANZANAR, CALIF.

THE SECRETARY OF WAR DESIRES ME TO EXPRESS HIS DEEP
REGRET THAT YOUR SON CORPORAL MAKOTO ASAI HAS BEEN
REPORTED MISSING IN ACTION IN FRANCE SINCE TWENTY-FIVE
OCTOBER IF FURTHER DETAILS OR OTHER INFORMATION IS
RECEIVED YOU WILL BE PROMPTLY NOTIFIED
ULIO THE ADJUTANT GENERAL

THEY SURE DO LOOK PEACEFUL.
SURE DO.
SEEMS A SHAME TO WAKE 'EM UP.
WE'RE AWAKE. THEY MIGHT AS WELL BE AWAKE TOO.
GOOD POINT.
HEY, RISE AND SHINE, SLEEPING BEAUTIES. UP AND AT 'EM, BOYS.
WHA...?
C'MON, DAD. JUST A COUPLE MORE MINUTES.

MAN INSIDE SAYS YOU BOYS ARE LOOKING FOR THE FRONT.
YES, SIR.
I'M HEADING BACK UP WITH A RECONSTRUCTED PLATOON. YOU'RE WELCOME TO TAG ALONG.
THANK YOU, SIR.
ONE THING-- AT SOME POINT I'M GOING TO WANT YOU TO SEPARATE FROM THE PLATOON LICKETY-SPLIT.
SEPARATE, SIR?
YEP. THAT JEEP IS GONNA DRAW MORTAR FIRE LIKE FLIES TO A COW PATTY. SO WHEN THE ROUNDS START DROPPING ON US THAT'LL BE YOUR SIGNAL TO PULL AHEAD. UNDERSTOOD?
UH, YES, SIR.
GOOD. SEE YOU ROUND THE OTHER SIDE OF THE CHURCH IN FIFTEEN MINUTES.

ATER...
Y'KNOW, MAK, I'VE BEEN THINKING.
CAREFUL--DON'T WANT TO HURT YOURSELF.
HA, VERY FUNNY. ANYWAY, I WAS THINKING. THEY PROBABLY DON'T KNOW WHERE WE ARE.
WHO DOESN'T KNOW WHERE WE ARE?
WELL, EVERYBODY.

THINK ABOUT IT--LIEUTENANT MILLER DOESN'T CARE ABOUT ANYBODY BUT HIMSELF. RIGHT?
TRUE.
AND NOW THAT HE GOT HIS BELL RUNG BY THAT SNIPER, DO YOU THINK HE'LL REMEMBER TO REPORT OUR WHEREABOUTS TO COMMAND?
PROBABLY NOT.
AND IF HE HASN'T REPORTED WHERE WE ARE THEN THE ARMY THINKS WE'RE MISSING IN ACTION. OR WORSE, AWOL!
THAT'S SOME INTERESTING THINKING YOU'RE DOING THERE, HARRY.
I'M SERIOUS, MAK! GUYS ON THE FRONT LINE GET SHOT FOR GOING AWOL! WHAT SHOULD WE DO?

I GUESS WE COULD TURN AROUND. MAYBE HEAD ALL THE WAY BACK TO REGIMENTAL COMMAND. LET 'EM KNOW WHERE WE WERE, WHAT WE'VE BEEN DOING. THEN COME ALL THE WAY BACK UP HERE. WANNA DO THAT?
WELL, NO. BUT THE POINT REMAINS. THIS IS CRAZY. WE'VE BEEN CUT LOOSE FROM STANDARD OPERATING PROCEDURE.
YOU'RE RIGHT. SEEMS TO ME, THOUGH, THAT BEING CUT LOOSE *IS* THE STANDARD OPERATING PROCEDURE UP HERE.

YEAH,
BUT THINK ABOUT IT. WE COULD GET SHOT FOR DOING THE RIGHT THING.
THAT'S TRUE, TOO. BUT UP HERE WE COULD GET SHOT FOR ALL SORTS OF REASONS. I'D SAY WE ONLY HAVE ONE OPTION--FOLLOW OUR INSTINCTS. MY GUT SAYS GO FORWARD. WHAT'S YOURS SAY?
AW, F'CRYIN' OUT LOUD, MAK! I KNEW YOU'D SAY SOMETHING STUPID LIKE THAT. ALL RIGHT, FINE. I AGREE-- WE GO FORWARD.
HOLD ON. DID YOU HEAR THAT?
HEAR WHAT?

INCOMING!
TAKE COVER!
GO, MAK, GO!
WHAM

WHAM!
YOU OKAY?!
I'M FINE! WATCH WHERE YOU'RE GOING!

WHAM!
WHAM!

WHAM!

I THINK THEY STOPPED. YOU ALL RIGHT?
UH, YEAH. BUT YOU'RE NOT. LOOKIT YOUR LEG!
WHAT THE...!
DOES IT HURT?
UH, NO, NOT REALLY. I DIDN'T NOTICE IT TILL YOU POINTED IT OUT.
WHAT SHOULD WE DO?
WELL, WE GOTTA GET IT OUT.

ARE YOU SURE WE SHOULD TAKE IT OUT?
NO, HARRY. I'M NOT SURE! BUT I CAN'T WALK AROUND WITH THIS TWO-BY-FOUR STICKING OUT OF MY LEG!
I KNOW THAT. I JUST THOUGHT MAYBE WE SHOULD GO BACK TO THE HOSPITAL AND LET THEM DO IT.
WE'RE NOT GOING BACK THERE FOR THIS.
I NEED YOU TO PULL IT OUT, HARRY. I'D DO IT MYSELF BUT I MIGHT MAKE IT WORSE.
OH, NO! NO, SIR! I'M NOT GONNA--
IT'S STARTING TO HURT. YOU GOTTA PULL IT OUT. C'MON, HARRY. DO IT!
I... I REALLY DON'T WANT TO DO THIS, MAK.

JUST DO IT, HARRY!
ALL RIGHT!
GAAA!
SORRY! SORRY! SORRY!
OH, MAN! NOW IT'S REALLY STARTING TO HURT.
SORRY. SORRY. SORRY.
STOP APOLOGIZING. IT'S NOT YOUR FAULT.
I KNOW. I JUST FEEL BAD FOR YOU. OH BOY, IT'S STARTING TO BLEED.
YES, I CAN SEE THAT.

LISTEN, HARRY-- YOU'VE GOT TO LOOK INTO THE WOUND. MAKE SURE THERE ARE NO SEVERED VEINS. NO SPLINTERS.
OH, I CAN'T DO THAT.
HARRY!
OKAY. OKAY. I'LL DO IT!
UHN... GRRR...
OH, BOY. SO... THAT'S... THAT'S MUSCLE AND THAT LOOKS LIKE BONE. OH, I'M GONNA PUKE.
HARRY!
OKAY, OKAY! SORRY. UH, I DON'T SEE ANY SPLINTERS. AND THERE'S NO BLOOD SPURTING SO NO SEVERED VEINS, I GUESS.
GOOD.
NOW GRAB A FIRST AID KIT. PUT SOME OF THAT SULFA POWDER ON IT AND WRAP IT TIGHT.
THERE. DONE.
HOW'S THAT?

HEY.
THIS FEELS GOOD.
I THINK I CAN WALK
ON IT. THANK YOU,
HARRY.
WELL, WHAT D'YA KNOW. I'M A MEDIC.
MEDIC,
MECHANIC--IT'S
ALL THE SAME.
RIGHT?

LET'S GO.
MAK,
YOU GOT A BIG HOLE IN
YOUR LEG.
ARE YOU
SURE YOU STILL WANT TO
DO THIS?

STOP
GOOFING AROUND, HARRY, AND
LET'S GO.
YOU DRIVE.

20. STANDARD OPERATING PROCEDURE

I didn't see the telegram about Mak, but it wasn't hard to tell that something was wrong. On the morning that it arrived, I had been out with Father gathering our laundry. When we returned, I saw that Mama was crying. I hugged her and she smiled. Then she asked me to go to the mess hall and get her a bowl of soup. That was strange. All the way there I kept wondering, *Why does Mama want soup? She doesn't even like soup.* When I got back, I hugged her again and she told me it was time for our nap. Mama left the soup untouched. We lay down together and Father went out. When we got up, she asked if we might just read for a while. I nodded and we read our own books. Eventually she just sat by my bed, looking out the window and rocking back and forth. Father kept walking in and out of the barracks. He'd come in, see Mama, look like he was going to say something, and then walk back outside.

If I'd seen even just the outside of the telegram, I would've known that something bad had happened to Mak. Everybody in the camp knew that telegrams from the army were bad news. They always had something terrible to say about the people you loved. Sometimes the telegram was brought to your barracks, and other times you'd be called to the administrator's office. One time a nurse called one of the kids out of the classroom to tell her that her parents had gotten a telegram. I remember hearing her start to cry and watching her through the classroom window as she ran home. Nobody wanted to receive a telegram.

It was right around when we got this telegram that I started thinking that maybe I might start talking again. I really wanted to. If only because of the look on Mama's face. I wanted to tell her not to cry. But honestly, I was afraid. I really felt by then that if I started talking before Mak got home, I would be responsible for whatever bad thing happened to him. I know it was a weird thing to think, but I couldn't help it.

And by then I'd grown so used to being silent that it seemed very strange to have words come out of my mouth. Since Mak had left, I'd spoken only a few times, and each one of those times I wasn't even aware that I'd talked until after I'd done it. I guess I was also afraid that if I tried to talk again, all that would come out of me were bird noises, like the night I wore the camouflage. And I never wanted that to happen ever again. For the time being, all I knew was that Mama and Father were acting stranger than usual.

The next day I decided to take a little stroll on my own. I hadn't done this in quite a while and didn't know what the response to my request would be. If I had known what was going on, I would've stayed. But as it was, the atmosphere in our room was stifling. Not with heat or even dust, but with the mood Mama was in. She was sitting by the window in our barracks, a cup and saucer on her lap. She would stare at the cup for a minute or two and then look back out the window. I'd tried getting her interested in reading or even playing a game of go fish. But she would just smile in a sad way, hug me, and turn back to the window.

So I decided to go for a walk on my own. Just a little one. I stood in front of Mama and waved my sketchbook back and forth, then cranked my thumb toward the door. Mama looked at me, smiling sadly.

"You want to go out?" she sighed.

I nodded.

"Well, all right. But be careful and don't go far. Come back in an hour."

Well, that was easy. I hurriedly grabbed my pencils, hugged Mama, and left, doing so as quickly as possible so I could be out of the barracks before Father got back and found some chore for me to do.

I walked down the main road toward the front gate. I don't know why. It just seemed like the right direction to go. The wind was blowing and dust swirled about my legs. Even when the camp was full to the brim, it could feel empty and forgotten. But now, with so few people left, it took on the look of one of those lonely ghost towns in a western movie. I expected John Wayne to come striding down one of the side alleys, pointing at me. *This here camp ain't big enough for the two of us,* he'd say, and I'd just have to pull my six-shooter from my holster and plug the varmint before he got the drop on me. Lucky for John

Wayne, I didn't have a six-shooter and he'd never be sent to Manzanar.

Gangs of tumbleweeds raced down the road toward me. One of them peeled away from the pack and veered in my direction. Just as it was about to run into me, I stepped aside, flourishing my sketchbook like it was the cape of a Spanish bullfighter. I heard someone clapping and looked up to see an old man sitting in the doorway of his barracks. I curtsied and he continued to clap.

"Toro! Toro!" he said, laughing.

I waved and continued walking.

Up ahead I could see that a bus had pulled past the guard posts and into the camp itself. It sat by the flagpole across from the administration building. Its baggage door was open, and people were putting their bags into it. More people leaving us.

As I got closer, I noticed two things: One, the bus had one of the weird dog designs on its side, like the bus that had taken Mak off to war. It was just as goofy-looking now as it had been then. And two, there were a couple of boys standing among the grown-ups by the bus. One of the boys looked in my direction. It was Sydney. He smiled, waved, and started walking toward me. I felt a little nervous. What would I say to him? But then I laughed at this thought. Of course, I wouldn't have to say anything. I'd made a vow of silence. I didn't have to talk to anybody. It was funny that after so long there were still times when I'd forget.

"Hey," he said. "Thanks for coming to see us off."

Hmmm, I thought, *do I write him a note telling him that*

I didn't come to say goodbye, but was only going for a walk and happened to arrive just as they were leaving? Or do I just smile? I smiled.

"So listen, do you wanna be pen pals? Y'know, I write you a letter and you write me back? No big deal. Just pen pals."

I didn't expect that. It wasn't bad that he asked me to be his pen pal—it was a good feeling, actually. I was just surprised. I didn't know what to do. I wanted to nod and smile like I usually did, but somehow that didn't seem like enough. Instead I opened my sketchbook and showed him a drawing. It was one of the drawings of Oba-chan bear sitting on the giant purple heart medal. Sydney took my sketchbook and held it for a moment.

"Wow!" he said at last. "Yeah. You were always a good drawer. The best in the class. Oh yeah, this is real good."

Sydney handed the book back to me, and we stood there for a while. When he started to make little lines in the dirt with his shoe, I opened the sketchbook and wrote, *I don't know where we're going,* and showed it to him. He read it, then looked at me, a little puzzled.

"So wait, does that mean you wanna be pen pals?"

I nodded.

"Hey, that's great! And don't worry about not knowing where you're going, 'cause I know where we're going. Can I borrow your pencil?"

I handed him a pencil, and Sydney opened my sketch-book to the back, where he wrote on an unused sheet of paper. I liked that; that he was kind enough not to write on a page that I'd already drawn on. I looked at what he'd written—his name and an address. It was a bit messy, but I could read it.

"Syd!" called a man over by the bus. "C'mon! We're going!"

"I'm coming!" called Sydney over his shoulder. "So you'll write to me?"

I nodded and smiled.

"Aw, that's swell! And I'll write back. Promise!"

Sydney put out his hand. I took it and we shook. Then he began running back to the bus. Halfway there, he stopped.

"G'bye, Mari! You're as beautiful as your art!"

I put my hand to my mouth and giggled. I'm not a big giggler, but I couldn't help it. Something was bubbling up inside me, something that made me want to laugh. Sydney ran on, stopped at the door, waved, and jumped on the bus. The engine revved and smoke billowed from the back. The bus lurched forward and started toward the gate. Once again the windows were too dirty to see anyone inside. That didn't matter. I stood there and waved as the bus passed the front gate and made its way down the highway toward St. Louis.

When the bus was out of sight, I walked back to our barracks. I stopped once and opened my sketchbook to look at Sydney's name and address. It was still there. I know it's funny to think it wouldn't be, but I just had to check.

When I returned, Mama was still sitting by the window.

"Mari," she said, "you're back. I was getting worried."

I put my arm around her shoulders and hugged her. She

felt smaller somehow. Or maybe I was bigger. Mama smiled and stood.

"Come along, my little suzume. Let's go to the mess hall. Father will meet us there for dinner."

We walked hand in hand to the hall. All the way I noticed that same strange sensation I'd felt when Sydney said goodbye the first time, like everything was fine and was going to stay that way. The air smelled sweet and Mama's hand felt good in mine. I took a deep breath, and once again I felt like my lungs were bigger, freer. *That's it,* I thought, *I'm happy again!* Was it odd to have become so used to feeling unhappy that feeling happy seemed strange and a little frightening?

Inside, Father was already seated and eating. He stood when we arrived at the table with our trays.

"I am sorry," he said, "I was so hungry, I just couldn't wait."

Father tried to start conversations with Mama, but she remained quiet. She ate very little.

"Mari, you've been smiling since you came in," Father said to me. "Are you okay?"

I just smiled at him and continued eating, but what I wanted to do was laugh or get up and sing and dance. It was a giddy feeling. I felt as if a little smile had been painted on the inside of me and wouldn't go away.

Western Union Telegram
10/27/44
To: MR. ICHIRO ASAI
MANZANAR, CALIF.

CONCERNING THE STATUS OF YOUR SON CORPORAL MAKOTO ASAI FURTHER INVESTIGATION INDICATES THAT HE MAY HAVE BEEN TRANSFERRED TO ANOTHER ASSIGNMENT ANXIETY CAUSED YOU BY THE PREVIOUS TELEGRAM IS REGRETTED AND FURTHER INVESTIGATION CONTINUES YOU WILL BE INFORMED OF THE RESULTS TO PREVENT POSSIBLE AID TO OUR ENEMIES AND TO SAFEGUARD THE LIVES OF OTHER PERSONNEL DO NOT DIVULGE ANY INFORMATION IN REGARD TO YOUR SONS BATTALION PORT OF EMBARKATION/ DEBARKATION OR ASSIGNMENT
ULIO THE ADJUTANT GENERAL

WAIT...
YOU HEAR THAT?
WHAT? THE MACHINE GUN FIRE?
NO. NOT THAT. IT SOUNDS LIKE...
MORTAR ROUNDS!
STOP! WE GOTTA FIND SOME COVER!

GO! RUN FOR THAT DUGOUT!
YOU OKAY?!
I'M GOOD! GO!

I HOPE THERE AIN'T NO BEARS IN THERE, MAK.
OH F'CRYING OUT LOUD, HARRY! GO IN ALREADY.
ALOHA. AIN'T NO BEARS IN HERE. JUST THIS BUDDHAHEAD.
WHOA! WHERE'D YOU COME FROM?
BEEN HERE THE WHOLE TIME, BRUDDAH.
HEY, YOU BOYS WOULDN'T HAPPEN TO BE THE REINFORCEMENTS I'VE BEEN CALLING FOR?
US? REINFORCEMENTS? HEH, THAT'S FUNNY. NO, WE'RE NOT YOUR REINFORCEMENTS.

WELL, IF YOU AIN'T REINFORCEMENTS, WHAT ARE YOU, THEN?
WE'RE HERE TO GET THE WOUNDED.
SO, YOU'RE MEDICS.
NO, WE'RE MECHANICS.
GETTIN' CROWDED IN HERE.
HEY, GEORGIE, SAY HELLO TO THE MECHANICS. THEY'RE HERE TO GET THE WOUNDED.
HELLO, MECHANICS.
CAN YOU TELL US WHERE YOUR WOUNDED ARE GATHERED?
ME? NAH. I'M JUST A RUNNER.
WHERE'S YOUR COMMANDING OFFICER?
HE'S DEAD.

WELL, WHO'S IN CHARGE, THEN?
THE SERGEANT.
WHERE IS HE?
UP THE HILL. I'M ABOUT TO HEAD BACK UP. YOU CAN FOLLOW ME IF YOU WANT.
THANK YOU.
NO SWEAT.
ON THE DOUBLE, BOYS. MORTARS WON'T STAY QUIET FOR LONG.
YOU GONNA BE ALL RIGHT?
YEAH. FEELS BETTER FOR SOME REASON. LET'S GO.

UH... OH... I-I CAN'T...
HE LOOKS PRETTY BAD.
HOLD ON, GEORGIE. WE GOT YOU.

WHAT DO WE DO NOW, MAK?
GIVE ME A MINUTE! I'M TRYING TO THINK.
WHERE'S... WHERE'S MY...MY HELMET?
LET'S GO BACK NOW, MAK! LET'S JUST PICK HIM UP AND BRING HIM BACK TO THE AID STATION.
NO!
WE'VE GOT ROOM FOR ONE MORE IN THE JEEP. I'M GOING TO GO SEE THIS SERGEANT. I'LL FIND OUT WHERE THE WOUNDED ARE AND BRING ONE DOWN. YOU STAY HERE WITH GEORGIE.
WAIT!
WHAT'S THE MATTER, GEORGIE?
WH-WHEN THE KRAUTS SHOT OUR CAPTAIN THIS MORNING, THE SERGEANT WENT A LITTLE CRAZY. HE GRABBED THE CAPTAIN'S THOMPSON MACHINE GUN AND CHARGED UP THE HILL, SCREAMING, "BANZAI!"

THE REST OF US...
THE REST OF US CHARGED UP THE HILL AFTER HIM.
THE KRAUT MACHINE GUN NEST AT THE TOP OF THE HILL HAD US PINNED DOWN HERE FOR THE PAST DAY AND A HALF. WE WIPED IT OUT IN NO TIME FLAT.
IT WAS THE MOST AMAZING THING YOU EVER SEEN.
A BANZAI CHARGE?
THAT'S RIGHT. THE THING IS, THE SERGEANT CAUGHT A GRENADE BURST IN HIS BELLY ON THE WAY UP THE HILL.
THE GRENADE TORE HIM UP PRETTY BAD. BUT HE WON'T LET NOBODY LOOK AT HIM AND HE WON'T GO BACK TO AN AID STATION.
LISTEN TO ME.
YOU GOTTA GET HIM TO AN AID STATION. HE DON'T DESERVE TO DIE OUT HERE.
I'LL DO MY BEST, GEORGIE.

WHERE'S YOUR SERGEANT?
THAT WAY.
NEXT BUNKER.
HOLD ON. WE'LL GIVE YOU SOME COVER FIRE.
GO!
WHERE'S YOUR SERGEANT?
SARGE! THE GUN'S TOO HOT! WE GOTTA LET IT COOL.
ALL RIGHT. BREAK OUT ANOTHER BOX OF AMMO.
I'MA TAKE A SEAT FOR A MINUTE. MY BELLY IS KILLING ME.

I'M LOOKING FOR THE SERGEANT.
YOU FOUND HIM. WHAT D'YA WANT?
WAIT. WHITEY?
THAT'S MY NAME! WHAT. DO. YOU. WANT?!
WHITEY, IT'S ME.
OH YEAH, WELL, WHO ARE YOU?

IT'S MAK, WHITEY. DON'T YOU RECOGNIZE ME?
MAK? JEEZ, MAK! WHAT ARE YOU DOIN' UP HERE?
I'M RETRIEVING THE WOUNDED.
SO, YOU'RE A MEDIC NOW?
NO, I'M A... FORGET ABOUT THAT. LISTEN, WHITEY, WHEN DID THIS HAPPEN TO YOU?

WHEN DID WHAT HAPPEN?
WHITEY, YOU'RE WOUNDED.
NO, I AIN'T.
HOLD ON. I GOTTA PUKE.
HEY, SARGE! THE GUN HAS COOLED!
I'LL BE RIGHT THERE!

GIMME A BREAK, WHITEY! YOUR STOMACH IS ALL SHOT UP AND YOU'RE VOMITING BLOOD.
IT'S NOTHIN'! I'M FINE!
NO, YOU'RE NOT, WHITEY. I'M TAKING YOU TO AN AID STATION.
OH MAN, I GOTTA PUKE AGAIN.
I'M TAKING YOU DOWN THE HILL, WHITEY.
LEAVE ME ALONE, MAK!

LET'S GO, WHITEY.
I'M NOT GOING TO NO AID STATION!
SARGE IS LEAVING? WHO'S IN CHARGE?
YOU ARE.
AW, CRUD! I KNEW THIS WAS GONNA HAPPEN.
AKIMOTO! GET YOUR BUTT OVER HERE AND LOAD THIS WEAPON FOR ME!

STOP FIGHTING ME!
LEMME GO, MAK! THEY NEED ME UP HERE!
THAT BELLY WOUND IS GOING TO KILL YOU IF I DON'T GET YOU TO AN AID STATION.
HOW DO YOU KNOW?! YOU AIN'T A MEDIC! YOU'RE JUST A STUPID JEEP JOCKEY!
HARRY!
MAK! OVER HERE!
I'M GOING BACK UP TO MY MEN, MAK!
MAYBE SOMEDAY.
BUT RIGHT NOW YOU'RE GOING TO AN AID STATION.

I'VE GOT WHITEY.
HOLD ON! YOU MEAN OUR WHITEY?
OF COURSE. HOW MANY JAPANES AMERICAN GI'S DO YOU KNOW NAMED WHITEY?
HE'S THE SERGEANT WITH THE BELLY WOUND GEORGIE WAS TALKING ABOUT.
NO KIDDIN'.

HOW'S GEORGIE?
OKAY, I GUESS. I MEAN HE'S STILL BREATHING. AND HE'S GOT A PULSE.
GOOD. PICK HIM UP AND LET'S GO.

YOU WANT ME TO CARRY HIM?
I CAN'T CARRY GEORGIE. HE'S NEARLY TWICE MY SIZE.

WHOA!
YOU OKAY?
OH YEAH.
JUST ONE BIG PARTY OVER HERE.
JUST START PULLING HIM DOWN THE HILL AND LET GRAVITY DO THE REST.
HE'S NOT DOING TOO GOOD, MAK!
JUST KEEP COMIN', HARRY.
HEY! I CAN SEE THE JEEP!
YEAH. WE'RE IN LUCK. IT'S STILL IN ONE PIECE.

STUPID BRANCH.
STUPID HELMET.
A STUPID BRANCH KNOCKED MY STUPID HELMET OFF.
HELP ME GET THESE TWO STRAPPED TO THE JEEP, AND THEN GO BACK AND GET IT.
OKAY.
YOU'D BETTER STRAP ME DOWN 'CAUSE RIGHT AFTER I KICK YOUR FOUR-EYED BUTT, I'M GONNA HEAD RIGHT BACK UP TO MY MEN.

LET. ME. GO. THAT'S AN ORDER!
BE QUIET, WHITEY.
DON'T PAY ANY ATTENTION TO HIM. IT'S JUST THE LOSS OF BLOOD THAT'S MAKING HIM SAY STUPID STUFF.
I'M TRYING NOT TO, BUT HE SOUNDS PRETTY CONVINCING.
I'M GONNA HAVE YOU BOTH COURT-MARTIALED! THEN SHOT! THEN I'M GONNA KICK YOUR BUTTS!
I'M DONE. LET'S GET GEORGIE.
OKAY. THAT'LL DO IT.
HURRY UP AND GET YOUR HELMET.
WILL DO. IT'S JUST UP THE HILL. I'LL BE RIGHT BACK.
I WANNA GO BACK TO MY MEN!

WHAM!
OH... OH...

HARRY!

HARRY!
MAK! HELP!
I... I CAN'T SEE, MAK! CAN YOU HELP ME FIND MY HELMET?

I GOT DIRT IN MY EYES. I CAN'T SEE.
I GOTCHA, HARRY. YOU'RE GONNA BE OKAY.

MAK, CAN YOU GET THE DIRT OUT OF MY EYES?
JUST HOLD ON, HARRY. I'M TAKING YOU TO AN AID STATION. THEY'LL FIX YOU RIGHT UP.

HOLD ON, BOYS!
WE'RE GETTING OFF THIS STUPID MOUNTAIN!

THIS HURTS. THIS HURTS. THIS HURTS.
C'MON, LEG. JUST GET US DOWN TO THE AID STATION.

GERMANS!
WUMP!
WHAT DO I DO NOW?

GO FOR BROKE.

HERR LEUTNANT.
WAS?
HERR LEUTNANT!

BANZAI!

I CAN SEE SOME GI'S UP AHEAD. HANG ON, HARRY.

HEY, CAP! THERE'S A STRANGE LOOKIN' JEEP COMIN' DOWN THE HILL. COULD BE ANOTHER KRAUT DECOY.
SHOULD WE FIRE SOME WARNING SHOTS?
GO AHEAD, SERGEANT.

AIM HIGH, BOYS!

STOP! WE'RE AMERICANS!

BLAM!
HEY...
HEY, WAIT!

STOP SHOOTING!
THWACK!
MAK!

CEASE FIRE!

I SAID CEASE FIRE, YOU IDIOT!
BLAM!

WHAT PART OF "CEASE FIRE" DON'T YOU UNDERSTAND?

WELL, DON'T JUST STAND THERE. GO HELP THEM!
YES, SIR.
MAK?

HURRY UP! WE'RE SITTING DUCKS OUT HERE IN THE OPEN.

THEY DON'T LOOK TOO GOOD, CAP.
UUNH... UUNH...
WHAT DO YOU WANT ME TO DO?
HANG ON, BUDDY. WE'RE GONNA GETCHA SOME HELP.

PUT THE DRIVER INTO THE BACK OF THAT JEEP.
AND DRIVE THOSE WOUNDED MEN OVER TO THE AID STATION.
THE DRIVER AIN'T GOT NO PULSE, CAP.
MAYBE WE SHOULD JUST LEAVE HIM HERE FOR THE GRAVEDIGGER BATTALION.

WILL DO, CAP!
ARE YOU A MEDIC, O'REILLY?
WELL NO, SIR, BUT--
THEN SHUT YER YAP AND DRIVE THAT JEEP OVER TO THE AID STATION!
PRONTO!
YES, SIR.
TAKE IT EASY WITH HIM, WILLIE.
MIND YOUR OWN BUSINESS, JOE.

HOW LONG TILL WE GET TO THE AID STATION, MAK?
WE'LL BE THERE SOON, BUDDY. AND SORRY, BUT I AIN'T MAK.
HEY, RELAX, BUDDY.
WHERE'S MAK?
MAK?!

MAK!
CALM DOWN, WILL YA?

21. WETNESS AROUND HIS EYES

I didn't see the second telegram either. But I knew things had really gotten strange when I heard someone sniffling while we were sleeping the night after it arrived. I sat up in bed and realized that it was Father. The sniffling didn't sound like he had a cold. It sounded like he was quietly crying.

Mama was still asleep beside me. I got out of bed and went over to stand by Father. He was sitting in the dark at the table. In the dim light I could see wetness around his eyes. I'd never ever seen Father cry. He looked at me and, oddly, smiled through his tears. I smiled back, but then I looked at him with a question on my face. He'd grown very good at understanding what the looks on my face meant.

"I'm sorry that I have woken you. And I'm sorry that I am crying," he said quietly. "A father should be strong for his children."

I put my hand on his and gave him another questioning look. Father took my hand, stood, and we walked out of the barracks and sat on the steps. I looked up at the sky. The stars were fiercely bright.

I leaned against his shoulder. Father looked down at me and smiled again.

"You are a good girl, Mari, and I love you," he said. "I am sorry that I say that so infrequently to you."

Father hadn't said anything like that to me for quite a while. And I'm not sure that he said it all that often after. But this one time was enough for me. I hugged him. We walked back into the barracks, and I crawled back into bed next to Mama. Father picked up his chair, put it next to my side of the bed, and sat down. With Mama on one side and Father on the other, I soon fell asleep.

Western Union Telegram
11/6/44
To: MR. ICHIRO ASAI
MANZANAR, CALIF.

REGRET TO INFORM YOU YOUR SON CORPORAL MAKOTO ASAI WAS WOUNDED IN ACTION IN FRANCE ON TWENTY-EIGHT OCTOBER YOU WILL BE ADVISED AS REPORTS OF CONDITION ARE RECEIVED ULIO THE ADJUTANT GENERAL

MORNING, DR. SCHROEDER. DON'T GET UP.
MORNING, COLONEL. THANK YOU.

HOW'S YOUR PATIENT WITH THE STOMACH WOUND?
HE'LL LIVE. IF HE DOESN'T KILL HIMSELF FIRST.
KILL HIMSELF?
WELL, NOT LITERALLY. HONESTLY, HE SHOULD'VE BEEN DEAD WHEN HE CAME IN. I DON'T KNOW HOW HE STAYED ALIVE WITH ALL THAT SHRAPNEL IN HIS BELLY.
AND NOW THE FOOL KEEPS TRYING TO GET UP AND GET BACK TO THE FRONT LINE. VERY IRRITATING TRYING TO HELP A STOMACH WOUND HEAL WHEN IT WON'T LIE DOWN.
HOW'S YOUR NECK-WOUND PATIENT?
TOUCH AND GO AT FIRST. HE HAD ALMOST NO PULSE WHEN HE ARRIVED. THE SLUG NICKED AN ARTERY. THERE WAS MORE BLOOD ON THE FLOOR OF THE JEEP THAN INSIDE OF HIM.
I GOT SOME PLASMA PUMPED INTO HIM HE'S STARTING TO LOOK LESS LIKE A CORPSE.

ONE TRICKY PART, THOUGH--THE BULLET WAS WEDGED UP AGAINST HIS LARYNX. I DID MY BEST, BUT HIS LARYNX TOOK A BEATING. ONLY TIME WILL TELL IF HE'LL BE ABLE TO TALK AGAIN.
YOUR BEST IS ABOUT AS GOOD AS IT GETS, CARL. FOCUS ON THE FACT THAT YOU SAVED HIS LIFE.
THANK YOU, COLONEL. I'LL DO THAT.
AND SO WHAT'S THE NEXT STEP FOR YOUR PATIENT?
WELL, WE'VE DONE ABOUT ALL THAT CAN BE DONE FOR HIM HERE.
I HOPE TO GET HIM ON THE EARLIEST FLIGHT TO ENGLAND. GOOD FRIEND OF MINE THERE IS AN EAR, NOSE, AND THROAT SPECIALIST. HE SHOULD BE ABLE TO HELP HIM.
EXCELLENT WORK, CARL.

UH, EXCUSE ME, SIRS.
WHAT'S UP, MINORU? NOT ANOTHER JEEP FULL OF WOUNDED, I HOPE.
NO, SIR. IT'S THE STOMACH WOUND. HE'S TRYING TO GET UP AGAIN.
AGAIN?! IS THAT GUNG HO COWBOY STILL TRYING TO GET BACK TO THE FRONT?
NO, SIR. HE SAYS HE JUST WANTS TO BE NEXT TO HIS BUDDY.
WHICH ONE IS HIS BUDDY?
IT'S THE NECK WOUND, SIR. DOCTOR SCHROEDER'S PATIENT.
WHAT D'YA SAY, CARL? SHOULD WE ALLOW OUR PATIENTS A LITTLE QUIET TIME TOGETHER?
SURE.
JUST BE CAREFUL TO KEEP THE NECK WOUND CALM AND IMMOBILE, OKAY?
CALM AND IMMOBILE. WILL DO, DOCTOR.

LISTEN UP, SERGEANT. YOU OUT-RANK ME OUT THERE BUT IN HERE I'M TOP DOG. SO WHAT I SAY GOES. NOW, YOUR BUDDY IS IN ROUGH SHAPE. HE'S GOTTA STAY CALM AND QUIET. THOSE ARE DOCTOR'S ORDERS. ONE WRONG MOVE AND I'LL PUT YOU RIGHT BACK WHERE I FOUND YOU. GOT IT?
LOUD AND CLEAR. I'LL BE AS GENTLE AS A LITTLE LAMB. PROMISE.
OKAY. HERE WE ARE.
IS HE ASLEEP?
SHOULDN'T BE. I JUST LET HIM KNOW YOU WERE COMING OVER. BUT LIKE I SAID, HE'S PRETTY ROUGHED UP. THEY JUST TOOK A SLUG OUT OF HIS THROAT, SO HE CAN'T TALK.

I GAVE HIM A PENCIL AND SOME PAPER IN CASE HE'S GOT SOMETHING TO SAY.
JUST TAKE IT NICE AND EASY.
WILL DO.
HEY, MAK.
MAK, IT'S ME, WHITEY.
LISTEN. I JUST WANT TO SAY THANK YOU.
AND THAT I'M SORRY.
YOU SAVED MY LIFE AND I TREATED YOU REAL BAD.
REAL BAD.
I SURE AM SORRY.
AND I HOPE YOU CAN FORGIVE ME.

MAK.
CAN YOU HEAR ME?

WHAT'D HE WRITE?
UH, JUST ONE WORD.
WHAT'S IT SAY?
WELL, LOOKS LIKE THE FIRST LETTER IS A B. AND MAYBE THE SECOND LETTER IS AN A.
I CAN'T MAKE IT OUT.
HERE. YOU TAKE A LOOK.

CAN YOU READ IT?
WELL, WHAT'S IT SAY?
I THINK...

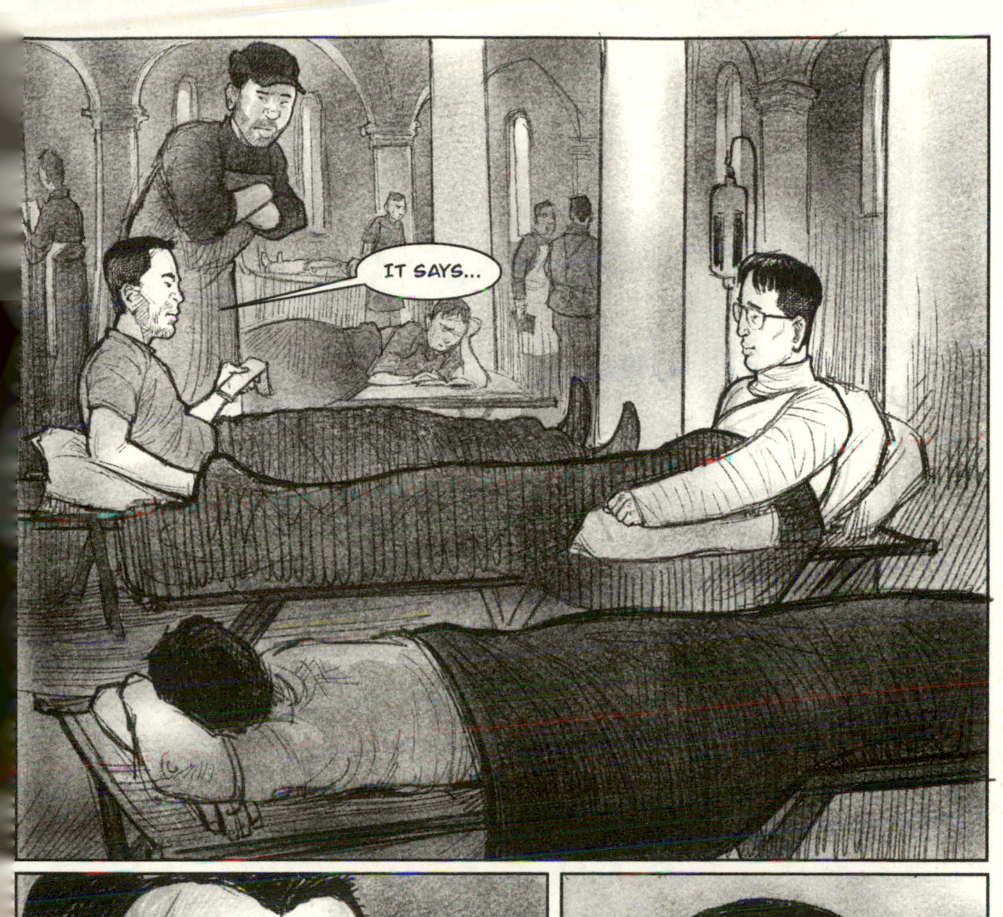
IT SAYS...

...BANZAI.

22. ONE PEG AT A TIME

Mama and Father were out when the person from the office brought the third telegram about Mak. It was just after supper. They had gone to a meeting where they were to learn more about acquiring passes for us to leave the camp. I was sitting at our barracks table, working on a crossword puzzle. I remember the clue to the word that I was stuck on: 23 across, "Southern general who led ill-fated charge at Gettysburg." I never finished that puzzle.

I remember hearing the knock on the door. I opened it and found a woman who I'd seen before but didn't know. She asked if Mama or Father was in. I shook my head. It was then that I noticed the telegram. I started to feel like I couldn't get enough breath into my lungs. I pointed at the telegram. She nodded her head slowly. At the time I thought her nod meant, *Yes, this telegram means your brother is dead.*

I know what you're thinking—*At this point Mari goes crazy again.* Well, I didn't. Okay, maybe I did a little. But I didn't turn into a bird again, if that's what you're thinking. But seeing that telegram definitely made me feel like life had taken a turn toward the unbearable. I couldn't stop staring at it. The lady was saying something, and all I could do was stare at the words printed in red across its top: WESTERN UNION TELEGRAM.

"Do you know where your parents are? This is very important."

I don't blame her for getting angry at me. At first I shook my head no because I didn't know exactly where they were. But then I recalled that the meeting to get the pass was in the school, so I started nodding yes. All the while I was staring at the telegram.

"Where are your parents?"

When she grabbed my arm, well, that was just too much. In order to put her hand on me, she had to take a step forward. And when she did, the telegram in her other hand loomed over me. I just had to get away from that telegram. I pushed past her and ran out into the night in my bare feet. It was windy, and a dust storm had kicked up after sunset. All I could think was, *Gotta find Mama! Gotta find Mama!* I ran up and down the streets, the wind and dust swirling around me. I looked up and became fascinated for a moment by how bright the stars were in spite of the dust storm. That's when I tripped over something and fell, scraping my knee.

The cut on my knee wasn't too bad, but I started crying anyway. And it wasn't just sniffles. I was sobbing—big, heaving sobs—because I couldn't find Mama and because of that foul telegram. And no matter how much I wanted to, I couldn't yell "Mama!" because I thought, *No matter what that telegram says, maybe if I stay silent, then Mak will be okay.*

Eventually I found myself standing by the camouflage factory. I don't know why. I'd had no intention of going there. I guess that's just where I seemed to end up when life got out of hand. The wind was still whipping up the dust, and the camouflage was making a lot of noise as it flapped about. As I think back on it now, it must've been an eerie sight, that abandoned camouflage factory at night in a dust storm. But this was my place, the place that nobody else wanted or even liked. Except the swallows. This was their place too, and I loved them. But even that thought wasn't enough to stop me from feeling very, very low. So I walked inside, thinking, *Too much*. And I knew that it wasn't just one particular thing that was too much. It wasn't just Manzanar. Or Oba-chan Yuki. Or Keiko. Or that telegram telling me Mak was dead. It was all of it. Every single bit of it.

Inside, I looked up at the rafters and the fluttering camouflage and found that, like me, the swallows were awake. I could see them, high above in the darkness, little gray dots darting back and forth. Most likely they were irritated by the wind and the dust. Or maybe they were just being neighborly and saying hello to their guest: me. I liked thinking of it that way. And I wanted to be up there with them.

I looked around and saw that there were pegs worked into the square wooden columns holding up the roof. The columns rose twenty feet from the ground and were met by the rafters, upon which the sparrows had built their nests.

I walked over and put my hand on one of the pegs and began climbing. And as I climbed, I thought, *I'm not a bird. I'm not a bird. I just want to sit up there with them. That's all.* My hands slipped from the pegs a few times. They were slippery from my wiping the tears and dust and snot from my face.

After a while—I'm not sure how long—I came to a high place where a rafter met the column I was climbing. I hoisted myself on top of the rafter and found a little nest resting there, but no swallows. *Isn't that nice,* I thought. *They've made a nest for me.* I tucked my feet under me and rested my back against the post.

Within a few minutes my thoughts turned from *This feels okay* to *I want to get down! I want to go home!* I hoped that getting down would be as easy as climbing up had been. It wasn't. Each time I'd move to maneuver myself into a position to put my hand or foot on a peg, I'd look down and get dizzy. Then I'd twist myself back up onto the rafter, too terrified to even consider moving. Soon I became so frightened that I felt myself start to freeze. My fear was turning me into stone. I didn't know what to do. So I arranged myself in such a way that I hoped, even if I should turn to stone, at worst I would stay there like a little rock high up in my nest of silence until Mama found me.

And that is what happened. After a long while or a little, I'm not sure, I heard Mama calling my name. It sounded very far away. But it was Mama and she was calling my name very clearly, like her life depended on my hearing her. Soon it seemed like she was very close.

“Mari!” I heard her say. “Mari! Are you here?”

I can’t move, Mama, I thought. *Come find me.*

“Mari,” said Mama. “Mak is not dead.”

My mind tried to work out what this could mean. Mama would not lie to me. But her news was so unexpected. *Mak is not dead.* It was like the sun had risen in the middle of the night and smiled at me.

“What?” I said. I was so shocked by what I’d heard that I forgot my vow again.

I could hear Mama take in a breath.

“Mari, Mak is not dead. He is hurt. But not dead.”

Now I had to get down! But what could I do? I was mostly frozen. It had taken a gigantic effort just to think my thoughts and move my mouth to say the word I’d said. Even though I could feel the warmth of this wonderful thought—*Mak is not dead*—weaving its way through the cold stone that I’d become, I began to worry. What would happen when I was no longer a frozen stone but wobbly me, perched on a rafter high above the ground? And then I found out. I took a deep breath, sobbed, and without thinking, rolled to my left and started to fall.

A few thoughts flitted through my mind as I fell from the rafter: *Father will say that this is abnormal* was the first thought. Then a wish popped into my mind: *Maybe Mama will catch me.* I knew that wasn’t likely. Lastly, I remember thinking: *What’s Father doing up here?*

I hadn’t heard or seen Father climbing the pegs on the column. But there he was. As I was falling past him, he grabbed my arm and swung me up against his side. He held me so tightly that it was a little hard to breathe. I didn't mind. It was just so nice not to feel like I was made of stone. Father didn't say a thing. He just held me close as he eased us down to the ground.

I hugged Mama, and we cried a lot, then went home to sleep.

11/28/44
US Army hospital
Norfolk, England
Dear Mari,

I am sorry that I've not written to you sooner. For the past few weeks I just haven't been able to get pen to paper. I know that you've probably been worrying about me, but please know that I am doing just fine. The wound I received was nothing serious. However, the doctors thought I could use a little time to rest up, so they sent me to an army hospital in England. My first flight on an airplane was quite an experience!

So here I sit in a cushy bed, wearing a swanky bathrobe over my crisp army pajamas. I feel great! I eat three square meals a day—mostly soft stuff like oatmeal because of my throat. Great doctors and nurses. And the hospital has its own swing band! I went to a dance last Saturday and had a swell time!
HEY, DOM. GET A LOAD OF WHAT JUST ROLLED IN!
HOLY SMOKES! A JAPANESE!

I'VE BEEN LOOKING TO TALK TO ONE OF THEM.
I WISH THEY'D TOLD US HE WAS GONNA BE HERE.
I WOULDA FOUND SOMETHING ELSE TO DO.
EXCUSE ME, NURSE. COULD YOU WHEEL ME OVER TO THAT JAPANESE FELLA?
CERTAINLY, SERGEANT.
ATTA BOY, DOM. GO GET HIM!
REMEMBER PEARL HARBOR.
CORPORAL ASAI HAS JUST HAD THROAT SURGERY SO HE CAN'T SPEAK.
NO KIDDIN'. WELL, I PLANNED ON DOING ALL THE TALKING ANYHOW.
CORPORAL ASAI.
THIS IS SERGEANT MCMANUS. HE'D LIKE TO HAVE A WORD WITH YOU.

HEY, MY NAME'S DOMENIC. YOU CAN CALL ME DOM. BUT, UH, I KNOW YOU AIN'T GONNA DO ANY TALKIN', SO I'LL KEEP THIS SHORT.
LISTEN, I JUST WANTED TO THANK YOU, ALL OF YOU, FOR WHAT YOUR REGIMENT DID FOR ME AND MY MEN.
CONSIDERING HOW MANY OF YOUR MEN WERE WOUNDED IN THE BATTLE, I THOUGHT I'D SEE LOTS OF YOU HERE IN THE HOSPITAL. BUT YOU'RE THE FIRST.
HOLD ON A SECOND.
YOU DON'T KNOW WHAT I'M TALKING ABOUT, DO YA?

YOU GOTTA BE WITH THE 442ND, THE GO FOR BROKE REGIMENT. AND I'M GUESSING YOU GOT THAT WOUND UP IN THE HILLS BEYOND BRUYÈRES.
BUT YOU DON'T KNOW WHY YOUR REGIMENT WAS UP IN THEM HILLS.
DO YA, CORPORAL?
I'LL BE DOGGONE.
I TELL YOU WHAT--I'M GONNA FILL YOU IN.
PLAIN AND SIMPLE, YOU JAPANESE BOYS SAVED ME AND MY BATTALION--THE 141ST INFANTRY, TEXAS NATIONAL GUARD. I JUST LEARNED THAT THE PAPERS HAVE STARTED CALLING US THE LOST BATTALION. WE WEREN'T LOST! WE WERE RIGHT WHERE OUR IDIOT GENERAL SENT US--SMACK-DAB IN THE MIDDLE OF THE GERMAN ARMY. DIDN'T TAKE LONG FOR THE KRAUTS TO FIGURE OUT WHAT WAS UP, AND THEY SURROUNDED US. OUR REGIMENT SENT HELP, BUT THEY COULDN'T GET THROUGH. WE WERE THERE FOR SIX DAYS AND NIGHTS. NO ARTILLERY SUPPORT. NO AIR SUPPORT. NO WAY TO GET OUR WOUNDED BACK TO AN AID STATION. JUST ABOUT THE WORST FIGHTING I EVER SEEN.

BY THE END WE WERE DOWN TO JUST ABOUT NOTHIN'. NO FOOD. DRINKIN' WATER OUTTA MUD PUDDLES. OUR AMMO ALMOST GONE. AIN'T NO WORDS TO REALLY DESCRIBE HOW DESPERATE IT WAS.
BUT THEN WE HEARD ON THE RADIO THAT A CRACK UNIT WAS COMIN' TO HELP US OUT. "HOLD ON!" THEY SAID, "THE **GO FOR BROKE** BOYS ARE COMIN'!" THAT NAME DIDN'T MEAN NOTHIN' TO ME UNTIL Y'ALL BROKE THE KRAUT LINE AND GOT THROUGH TO US. I REMEMBER ONE OF YOUR BOYS SHOOK MY HAND AND OFFERED ME A STICK OF GUM.

LEMME TELL YA, I WAS NEVER SO HAPPY TO SEE A JAP, I MEAN, A JAPANESE IN MY LIFE.
AND WOULDN'T YOU KNOW, IT WAS JUST MY BAD LUCK I STEPPED ON A MINE ON THE WAY BACK TO OUR LINES.

THE PARTY'S OVER, SERGEANT.
READY TO HEAD BACK TO THE WARD?
JUST WAIT. I GOTTA FINISH THIS.

THE THING IS, CORPORAL, I OWE YOU. HECK, MY WHOLE OUTFIT OWES YOU. IF IT WASN'T FOR THE 442ND, WE'D ALL BE IN A PRISON CAMP OR DEAD.
WHAT CAN I SAY BUT THANK YOU?

LISTEN, IF YOU EVER FIND YOURSELF IN GONZALES, TEXAS, JUST ASK FOR DOM IN THE FIRE DEPARTMENT.
YOU'VE GOT A BROTHER IN TEXAS AND THAT'S A FACT.
I'LL BE BACK FOR YOU IN A MOMENT, CORPORAL. YOU DON'T MIND, DO YOU? NOW THERE'S A GOOD FELLOW.
Please tell Pop that I got his letter. It's so good to hear that you'll be leaving Manzanar. I'm sorry that I missed spending Thanksgiving with all of you, but I'm hopeful that I'll be seeing you soon.
Love, your big brother Mak

23. HOME-FRONT COMMANDOS

First: Even though I broke my vow and said a few words before falling off that rafter, I decided not to beat myself up for failing to keep my silence again. That was an extreme circumstance. And a vow can be flexible under those conditions.

Second: We didn't leave when we thought we would. Both Mama and Father wanted to leave as soon as possible. But they couldn't agree on where we should go. And that's why it took so long for us to get going.

For weeks, well into the new year, all I remember is their arguing about where we should go. Father wanted to go back to the town where our farm had been. Mama wanted to go anyplace but there. And she was loud about her opinion on that. Louder than she'd ever been about anything. She couldn't stand the idea of going back to the place we'd left, knowing that the same people who'd written terrible things in the newspaper about us—well, not us personally, but Japanese Americans—were still there.

"I am a farmer, Aki. This is what I know. I want to go back to the place where we know the land, the weather. And also the people. They will take us back," said Father one night before bed.

I was sitting at the table next to Father. We'd been playing go fish. Mama stood with her hands on her hips, her hair down, staring out the window at the sun setting over the Sierras. I looked at Mama and I thought: *This is a different Mama.* She'd become stronger and sometimes angrier over the past few months.

"I received a letter today," she said as she turned to face Father. "It's from Mary Hayami. She and her husband, Sumio, left camp a little while ago. They went back to their farm."

"Yes, I remember them," said Father. "But let me stop you right there. I know what you are going to tell me—that they are having a difficult time. That they are not being accepted. Well, this will be something that all of us will have to overcome. It won't be easy, but we can do it."

Mama calmly sat down by the table. She reached into her purse and pulled out an envelope, from which she took a letter.

"'Dear Aki,'" read Mama, "'I am sorry to greet you with sadness, but this has been the emotion that has most been with me since our return home to our farm. When we arrived, we found that our home had been vandalized. Many of our things had been broken and strewn across our front yard. Some of our things had been thrown down our well. A neighbor told us that a truck full of men had shown up and done this after we'd been sent to Manzanar.'"

Mama put the letter down.

"There's more like this in the letter, Ichiro."

"Aki, no matter what that letter says, I still want to go home," said Father.

Mama reached into the envelope and pulled out another piece of paper.

"They found this on the windshield of their car when they came out of church," said Mama.

Mama handed the piece of paper to Father. It was a small poster. On it was a crude drawing of the face of what was supposed to be a Japanese man. He wore big glasses and had goofy-looking buckteeth. I'd seen drawings like this on billboards and in magazines before we left for Manzanar. Across the top of the little poster, in large black print, it said: SLAP THE JAP. Beneath that, a smaller line read, NO JAP IS FIT TO ASSOCIATE WITH HUMAN BEINGS. It was signed, THE HOME-FRONT COMMANDOS. Father looked at the poster for a moment, then at me.

"Mari should not see this," he sighed.

Mama took the poster, folded it, and put it and the letter back into the envelope, then into her purse.

"Yes, she should. And she might as well get used to it now, Ichiro, because that's where you want us to live," said Mama.

"Aki, what will I do? I am a farmer. If we don't go home, where will we go?"

Mama thought for a moment. She picked up her cup of tea and sipped.

"I don't know yet," she said. "But we are not going back there. Because that is no longer our home."

12/18/44
US Army hospital
Norfolk, England
Dear Mari,

You'll be happy to learn that the docs have allowed me to speak again. Mostly, I spend my days hanging out with my buddy Harry. Harry lost an eye back in France. I read to him and keep him entertained with my wit and charm. Ha!

WELL, LET'S SEE. UH, IT SAYS, "TWO HUNDRED SEVENTY AMERICAN INFANTRYMEN OF THE SEVENTH ARMY WERE RESCUED TODAY BY OTHER DOUGHBOYS WHO FOUGHT THEIR WAY THROUGH THE GERMAN ENCIRCLEMENT RING."
AND THEN WE GOT A LOVELY PICTURE OF A WHITE GI SHAKING HANDS WITH ANOTHER WHITE GI.
DOUGHBOYS BREAK GERMAN RING TO FREE 270 TRAPPED EIGHT DAYS
NOT A SINGLE KOTONK OR BUDDHAHEAD IN SIGHT.

WAIT A SECOND! IT DOESN'T SAY ANYTHING ABOUT US?
NOPE. NOT ONE MENTION OF THE 442ND. JUST A LOTTA TALK ABOUT THE LOST BATTALION AND THE "RELIEF UNIT" THAT SAVED THEIR BUTTS.
I CAN'T BELIEVE IT! HOW CAN THEY TREAT US LIKE THIS?!
AH, YOU KNOW THE OLD DRILL, HARRY. IT'S JUST STANDARD HAOLE JUNK IN A STANDARD HAOLE NEWSPAPER. RIGHT?
BUT IT AIN'T RIGHT, MAK! WE LOST TWO HUNDRED MEN UP THERE. AND AT LEAST EIGHT HUNDRED WERE WOUNDED! NOBODY'S GONNA KNOW WHAT WE DID!
YOU'RE PREACHING TO THE CHOIR, KIDDO.

HOW'RE YOUR FOLKS DOIN', MAK?! ARE THEY ENJOYIN' THE FRESH AIR AND CAMP LIFE AT MANZANAR? MEANWHILE, OUR REGIMENT GETS MARCHED INTO ONE MEAT GRINDER AFTER ANOTHER, AND WE DON'T EVEN GET A MENTION IN THE PAPER!

I'M SICK OF IT!

OH MY! IS EVERYTHING ALL RIGHT?
DON'T MIND HIM. HE'S JUST FEELING A LITTLE IRRITABLE.
CAN I GET YOU SOMETHING?
SURE! YOU CAN GET MY FAMILY OUTTA THE TULE LAKE INTERNMENT CAMP!

TOOLAH WHAT?
TULE LAKE, YOU DUMMY!
AND WHILE YOU'RE AT IT, YOU CAN FIND MY LEFT EYE AND STICK IT BACK IN MY HEAD!

YES, WELL, I THINK I SEE WHAT'S GOING ON HERE.
IT LOOKS LIKE SOMEONE NEEDS SOME MORE MEDICATION TO HELP HIM MIND HIS MANNERS. I'M GOING TO CALL THE DOCTOR.

HEY! HEY, WAIT!
YES, THAT'S EXACTLY WHAT I'M GOING TO DO.
I'M GOING TO GET YOU SOME MEDICATION TO CALM YOU DOWN.
HOLD ON! I'M SORRY. I DON'T NEED ANY MORE PILLS.

ARE YOU SURE? BECAUSE I CAN CALL THE DOCTOR AND HE'LL RAISE YOUR DOSAGE LICKETY-SPLIT.
NO, NO, YOU DON'T HAVE TO DO THAT.
I'LL CALM DOWN. I PROMISE. HONEST.
ALL RIGHT. BUT NO MORE OUTBURSTS. THIS IS A PLACE OF HEALING, NOT TEMPER TANTRUMS.
YEAH. SURE. I'M SORRY.

YOU OKAY?
YEAH. I'M FINE.
YOU BETTER WATCH IT, HARRY. THEY'LL PUT YOU IN THE PSYCH WARD FOR THAT KIND OF BEHAVIOR.
I KNOW. THAT WAS CLOSE. I GOTTA BE CAREFUL NOT TO LOSE IT LIKE THAT.
IT'D BE JUST MY LUCK.
I GET SENT TO A MENTAL WARD BECAUSE I'M A LITTLE IRRITATED ABOUT LOSING MY EYE AND MY FAMILY BEING STUCK IN A PRISON CAMP.
TELL YOU WHAT, MY LEG'S FEELING PRETTY GOOD TODAY. HOW ABOUT YOU AND ME ROLL OUT OF HERE AND GO FOR A STROLL AROUND THE JOINT?
SOUNDS GOOD. LET'S GO.

WHERE ARE YOU TWO GOING?
OUT FOR SOME FRESH AIR. WE'LL BE BACK IN A BIT.
YEAH. DON'T WAIT UP.
OKAY, WE'RE OUT. WHERE TO?
ANYWHERE BUT BACK IN THERE.
ALL RIGHTY. HOLD ON. HERE WE GO.
Anyway, I'm feeling good and hope to be well enough for travel soon. I'm guessing the wounds I received will be enough to get me a medical discharge. If that's so, then I may be on a boat for home! Keep your fingers crossed. Please take good care of yourself and keep an eye on the door. I may just walk through it sometime soon!
Love, your big brother Mak

24. A FAMOUS PLACE FOR CORN

I know what you're thinking: *Now that Mak is coming home, Mari is going to give up her vow of silence.* Well, you're wrong. Of course I didn't give up my vow! Think about it—even though Mak was coming home, he wasn't home yet. And that "yet" made all the difference. I had my part to do in this war too. And as silly as it may sound to you, I knew that my vow was at least part of what was keeping Mak safe. And until I saw him standing in front of me wearing his goofy glasses and all dressed up like a soldier, I was going to keep my mouth closed. And it wasn't easy. Even Mama brought up my vow of silence.

"I know it's important to you," Mama said to me one afternoon. "But with Mak coming home and us going off to find a new place to live, I think it might be a good time for you to consider talking again. It'd be a big help to Father and me."

It was late afternoon and the sun had already slipped behind the Sierras. In the gray light Mama looked very old. And very tired. We were sitting down together on our bed. I looked at the lines around her eyes. She had always been the one to help me through every little thing. Every big thing. Everything. But to ask this? *Maybe I should do it,* I thought. *Maybe I should give up my vow. That would help Mama.* I stood up, faced her, and was about to speak when Mama took my hand.

"Wait," she said.

Mama put her head down. I thought she was about to cry, but when she looked up, her eyes were dry and clear.

"I think I have asked this of you because I am tired. And afraid."

I felt my eyes start to flood.

"It would be easier if you talked, Mari. But let me ask you something. When you started, I think you chose to be silent for one reason or another, and yet for quite some time now I've believed you've been silent to keep your brother safe. Haven't you?"

I nodded slowly, tears slipping from my eyes.

"Then I have no right to ask you to stop. The easy way isn't always the best way. No matter how difficult it is for us or you. This is your choice and it is admirable. Thank you for protecting our Mak."

I hugged Mama. Since I was standing and she was sitting, her head rested on my shoulder, like I was the Mama and she the Mari. We cried like that for a little while. Then we lay down and took a nap until it was time for dinner.

A week later I came back to the barracks with a load of laundry to find Father packing his suitcase. Mama was sitting on their bed, a kerchief in her hands and tears on her cheek. Father had applied for a travel pass. The pass would allow him to travel back to our old farm and then return.

He wanted to get the money we'd made from the sale of our farm that we'd deposited in the bank in our hometown. He also wanted to retrieve some other things back at the farm.

"This is something I must do," said Father.

"Ichiro," replied Mama. "You don't have to go to the bank. No matter where we go—they can wire our money from our old bank to a new one. I asked at the front office. It is an easy thing to do."

"Maybe so," said Father, packing his socks, "but what about the things? The things I buried in the front garden before we left?"

"A few coins, Ichiro? Some photos and my old wedding kimono? We have lived without them all this time. We'll do just fine without them from now on."

Father turned toward Mama, an angry look on his face.

"My father gave me those coins when I left Japan. I will not leave them in the dirt."

Mama folded her hands on her lap and sighed.

"I cannot stop you from going. But I am frightened, Ichiro. I am frightened of what may happen to you. I am frightened about how the new owner may treat you when he finds you digging in his garden."

Father put his hand on Mama's shoulder.

"Aki, I'm not a fool. I won't just show up at the house with a shovel and start digging. I'll approach him with courtesy. I'll respectfully request to retrieve what is ours. I can't imagine anyone taking issue with that."

"I can," said Mama.

Father snapped his suitcase shut.

"It's time to go. Will you come with me to the front gate?"

"Of course," said Mama.

We walked through the camp. I was in the middle, Father on my left, Mama on my right. I started to feel pretty bad as we walked. Tears came to my eyes. This felt just like when Mak left. Even though Father wasn't joining the army, it felt like he was heading off to war. Who knew what would happen to him out there? When we finally came to the bus, Father put down his bag and bowed. Mama and I bowed back.

"I will be home in a week," he said.

"Travel safely," said Mama.

Father climbed onto the waiting bus. It was another bus with that strange drawing of a dog on its side. He sat down inside and waved to us as it drove off. We watched the bus churn up dust as it headed south, toward our old farm. After a few moments Mama took my hand and we walked to our barracks.

Father returned in less than a week. On the fourth night after he'd left, Mama and I were walking to our barracks after dinner when a neighbor called to us.

"Happy for you that Ichiro is back!" she said.

"What?" replied Mama.

"Ichiro is back. Didn't you know? He's in your barracks."

We ran to our barracks and flung the door open to find Father sitting at the table, his suitcase on the floor beside him. He looked very tired. There was a bruise under his right eye. He lifted his hand and tapped his finger on a piece of paper that was lying on the table.

"I got our money, Aki," he said. "I got the check from the bank."

I ran to him. I would've hugged him but Father didn't look like he wanted a hug from me at that moment. Mama sat beside him at the table.

"Thank you, Ichiro," she said.

Father, stoop shouldered, rubbed his hand over the stubble on his chin. Some of the hairs were white. He looked very old. I didn't remember him looking this old before. He looked at Mama, then out the window.

"I should've listened to you, Aki. It was just as you said it would be."

Mama rose, ladled some water from the basin into the teapot, and put it on the heater.

"I was threatened several times—on the bus there, in town, and on the way back. The people at the bank were rude. I thought for a while that they might not give me our money."

Father tapped the check on the table again.

"But I insisted. I stayed there and I insisted. And I got our money."

"Thank you, Ichiro," Mama said again.

"I went right to the bank and withdrew it. It's all right here in this check," said Father. "I wouldn't leave without it."

Father hung his head. He continued speaking, almost in a whisper.

"But that is all that I was able to retrieve, Aki. The new owner of our farm would not let me dig up our things. He said he would call the police on me if I did not leave. I am sorry."

"I am grateful that you tried, Ichiro. But I am even more grateful that you are safely here with us."

Mama poured tea for the three of us.

"On the last night I was there," said Father, "a man tripped me as I was leaving the diner where I'd eaten supper. I hit my face on a chair. People laughed and clapped."

Mama placed Father's tea in front of him. His hand shook as he picked up the cup, tea spilling on his lap. Watching this, I became very angry. I wanted to find those people who'd hurt Father and hurt them right back.

"You were right, Aki. I should've listened to you. That place is not our home. We can't go back there."

"Perhaps you'd like to lie down. We can talk more about this later," said Mama.

Father looked at Mama, then me. His eyes wore big circles under them. His face was droopy, like a hound dog's. He nodded slowly, stood, then walked over to the pan in which Mama had warmed water for tea and washed his face. I helped him take off his shoes, and Mama pulled down the sheets for his bed. He lay down stiffly, rolled over, and fell asleep in his clothes. I thought he was pretending. He'd started to snore in that way people do when they're pretending to be asleep. I tried to get him to sit up, but Mama stopped me.

"Let him rest," she whispered. "He'll be better in the morning."

The next morning Father slept through breakfast. He usually woke at sunrise. I wanted to get him up so he could come eat with us, but again Mama said we should let him sleep. When we returned, Father was up, dressed and shaved, and sitting at the table with a cup of tea and a big, open book in front of him.

"Good morning," he said in a cheery tone.

"You are feeling better today?" inquired Mama.

"I am," he replied. "Yes, I am. I got up this morning and realized that since we have the check with our savings, we can live anywhere we want. Anywhere at all! This made me feel wonderful. In fact, it still makes me feel wonderful."

Father smiled at us, rubbed his hands together, and clapped. I clapped too. He could be a lot of fun when he was in a good mood.

"And then I thought—if we're going to make an informed decision on where would be the best place for us to live, we'll need to educate ourselves! So I went right over to the school and borrowed this book—an atlas, a lovely book filled with wonderful maps! Especially this map."

Father placed both hands on the book and pulled it closer. It was open to a map of the continental United States. Gently he ran his hands over the map, as if he could feel the mountains, rivers, and valleys under his fingers.

"Look at this map with me, Mari. Go ahead—choose a place. Anyplace at all. As long as it's east of Manzanar and it's got good farmland. Go ahead, maybe we'll move there!" he said.

I didn't much feel like playing this game. I'd never had a fondness for maps. In fact, they were confusing to me. But I wanted to help keep Father in this happy frame of mind, so I leaned over the map and scanned the names of cities and states. I was about to pick a city with a name that sounded interesting to me and had my finger hovering over "Cincinnati" when Father put his finger down elsewhere on the map.

"Omaha, Nebraska!" he shouted. "That sounds like a wonderful place. Oh, I've heard of Nebraska—a famous place for corn. A wonderful place for farmers like us!"

Mama stood to one side, watching Father as he walked about our barracks. It looked as if he was imagining himself marching around his Nebraska cornfields. Mama opened Father's suitcase, began removing his dirty clothes and putting them in the laundry basket.

"Omaha could be a good place," said Mama. "But I will want us to consider other places before we choose our new home."

"Aki," said Father, his brow furrowing. "Omaha is the perfect place for us. I am certain of it."

Mama picked up the basket of dirty laundry and headed for the door. I followed her, not wanting to be left behind with Father, as his happy mood appeared to be departing.

"We'll do some more research when we return with the laundry," said Mama.

"Omaha, Aki. I'm certain of it," I heard Father say as the door closed behind us.

1/10/45
US Army hospital
Norfolk, England
Dear Mari,

I hope you had a happy Christmas and that all are doing well. I am feeling much better. And I'm happy to say that my friend Harry is on his way back to the States. The doctors want him to be in a hospital back at home for any future surgery on his eyes. I was sad to see him leave but have high hopes for his recovery. I wish I could say that I, too, were on my way home, but I can't. It seems that Uncle Sam isn't ready to let me out of this army. This is sad news, I know. But this is the way things sometimes are for a soldier. I had thought my wounds would be my ticket home. But I was wrong. I'm sorry I got your hopes up, Mari.

THEY'VE GOTTA BE KIDDING.

I CAN'T BELIEVE THIS!

MIND IF I JOIN YOU?
HUH? UH, NO, FATHER. GO AHEAD AND TAKE A SEAT. BUT I'M NOT GOING TO BE VERY GOOD COMPANY RIGHT NOW.
WHY? DID YOU GET A DEAR JOHN LETTER?
DEAR JOHN LETTER? ME? NOT LIKELY.
YOU GOTTA HAVE A GIRLFRIEND TO GET DUMPED BY ONE OF THOSE LETTERS. AND I CERTAINLY DON'T HAVE A GIRLFRIEND.
THEN I'M GUESSING THOSE MUST BE ORDERS SENDING YOU BACK TO THE FRONT.
THAT'S RIGHT. HOW'D YOU KNOW?
WELL, YOU'RE NOT THE ONLY WOUNDED GI TO GET ONE OF THOSE NOTICES TODAY.

YOU'RE CORPORAL MAKOTO ASAI, MECHANIC WITH THE 442ND.
YOU WERE AT THE FRONT DURING THE LOST BATTALION CAMPAIGN. YES?
YEP. THAT'S ME.
I WAS WITH THEM JUST LONG ENOUGH TO GET SHOT IN THE NECK.

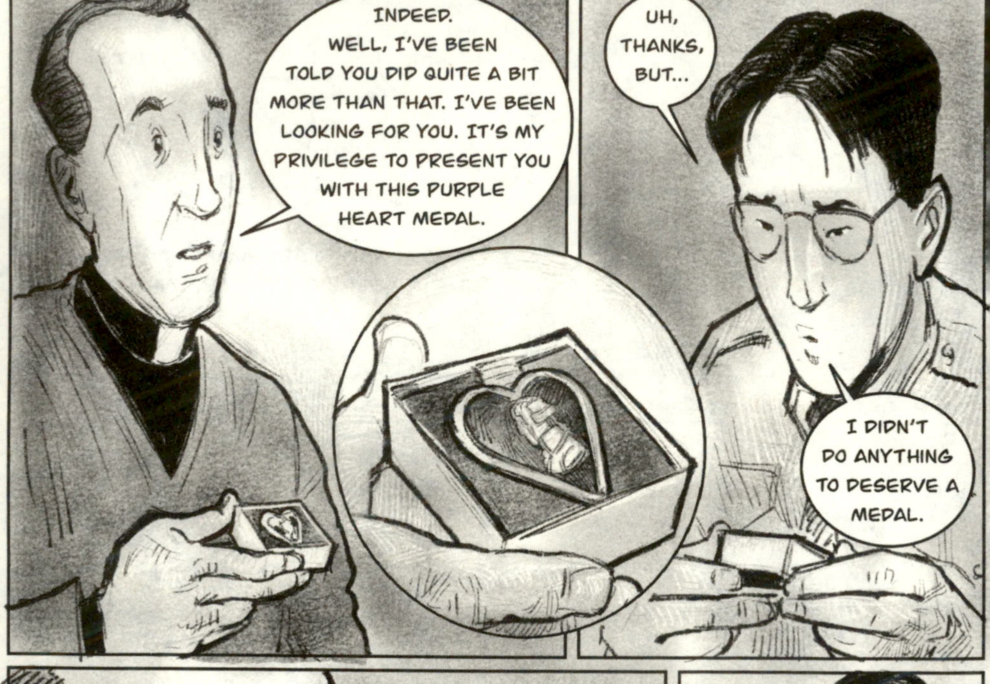
INDEED. WELL, I'VE BEEN TOLD YOU DID QUITE A BIT MORE THAN THAT. I'VE BEEN LOOKING FOR YOU. IT'S MY PRIVILEGE TO PRESENT YOU WITH THIS PURPLE HEART MEDAL.
UH, THANKS, BUT...
I DIDN'T DO ANYTHING TO DESERVE A MEDAL.

IN THE PROCESS OF SAVING TWO MEN'S LIVES--AND ATTEMPTING TO SAVE ANOTHER--YOU WERE SERIOUSLY WOUNDED IN THE THROAT AND LEG. SON, I'D SAY YOU DESERVE THAT MEDAL AND A LOT MORE.
WELL, AGAIN, THANKS.

I ALSO HAVE THIS FOR YOU.
WHAT'S THIS?
IT'S A PROMOTION. YOU ARE NOW SERGEANT ASAI OF THE AMBULANCE CORPS.
ME? A SERGEANT IN THE AMBULANCE CORPS?!
THIS IS WHAT I GET FOR LETTING THEM WELD THOSE STRETCHERS TO MY JEEP.
PERHAPS. BUT I HAVE A FEELING THAT PROMOTION ALSO HAS A LOT TO DO WITH YOUR COURAGE AND RESOURCEFULNESS.
LET ME INTRODUCE MYSELF.
MY NAME IS LEWIS POWERS. YOU CAN CALL ME FATHER LEW.

PLEASED TO MEET YOU, FATHER LEW. YOU CAN CALL ME MAK.
THE PLEASURE'S MINE, MAK.
CAN I BE STRAIGHT WITH YOU, FATHER?
ABSOLUTELY.
I DON'T SEE HOW I'M GOING TO DO ANYBODY ANY GOOD BACK AT THE FRONT.
I MEAN, I CAN BARELY SPEAK. I FEEL LIKE I'VE BEEN RUN OVER BY A TRUCK. I JUST WANT TO GO HOME.
Y'KNOW, MAK, I KNOW JUST HOW YOU FEEL.
ABOUT SEVEN MONTHS AGO, WHILE CRAWLING AROUND ON OMAHA BEACH, I HAD THE UNPLEASANT EXPERIENCE OF BEING SHOT IN THE BUTT. THAT'S RIGHT--THE BUTT. AFTER BEING EVACUATED TO THIS HOSPITAL, I SPENT QUITE A BIT OF TIME FACEDOWN ON A COT. THEN I SPENT MONTHS LIMPING ABOUT ON CRUTCHES. THANKS TO GOD, I AM NOW, AS THEY SAY, AMBULATORY.

WAIT.
YOU WERE ON THE BEACH ON D-DAY?
YEP. JUST DOING MY JOB, TENDING TO THE SPIRITUAL NEEDS OF MY BOYS WHILE WE CRAWLED ABOUT IN ABSOLUTE HELL. I DON'T MIND TELLING YOU THAT MY FIRST THOUGHT AFTER BEING SHOT WAS *THANK YOU, GOD, I'M GOING HOME.* THAT'S NOT THE FIRST TIME I MISINTERPRETED GOD'S PLANS FOR ME.

AND NOW THAT I'M FINALLY UP AND ABOUT, I'VE FOUND THAT THE ARMY HAS OTHER PLANS FOR ME AS WELL.
THEY'RE NOT SENDING YOU BACK TO THE FRONT TOO?!

EVENTUALLY. RIGHT NOW THEY HAVE SOMETHING ELSE IN MIND--FOR BOTH OF US.
WHAT DO YOU MEAN "US"?
YOU AND I WILL JOIN THE 442ND LATER. RIGHT NOW YOU'LL SPEND ANOTHER MONTH IN REHABILITATION. FOLLOWING THAT, BOTH OF US WILL BE GIVEN A CRASH COURSE IN FIELD MEDICINE.
I'M NOT A MEDIC. I'M A MECHANIC.

YOU HAVE A TALENT FOR HELPING PEOPLE WHO ARE HURT. THE ARMY DOESN'T WASTE TALENT.
I DON'T KNOW A THING ABOUT MEDICINE!
THINK ABOUT IT THIS WAY, MAK--YOU'LL STILL BE RESPONSIBLE FOR A VEHICLE. THE ARMY ISN'T TAKING ANYTHING FROM YOU. THEY'RE GIVING YOU SOME NEW TRAINING AND RESPONSIBILITY.
THE ARMY IS SWELL THAT WAY.
LET'S NOT FORGET THAT TICKET BACK TO THE FRONT THEY'RE GIVING ME.
YES, WELL...
...THERE'S THAT, TOO.

I'M SORRY. I'M NOT ANGRY AT YOU, FATHER. IT'S LIKE I SAID-- I JUST WANT TO GO HOME.
YOU'RE NOT THE ONLY ONE, MAK. ME AND ABOUT A HALF MILLION OTHER GI'S ARE RIGHT THERE WITH YOU.

I know that Mom and Pop are looking for a new place for you to live. Please give them my love and tell them to find a place that is sunny but not too hot. And make sure to remind them that wherever you go, I'll find you when this is all over.

I miss you, kiddo. Don't forget to give yourself some noogies now and then!

Love, your big brother Mak

25. TWENTY-FIVE DOLLARS FOR THREE YEARS

Mak didn't come home like he said he would. When I got his letter telling me that he had more things to do for the army before he could come home, I tore it right up. Then I felt bad about that, gathered all the pieces of the letter, and went to the office, where they let me have some tape. I was crying as I taped the letter back together, so some of the words got blurred. By the time I was through with it, the letter was a big mess. I've kept it with all his other letters. But it's a taped-up, blurry mess.

I was a mess too. I cried through the afternoon. During all the time he'd been gone, I'd tried to push the thought of never seeing Mak out of my mind. Sometimes I was able to do that. Sometimes not. That afternoon was one of those times when I just couldn't stop thinking about losing him. I kept hearing a voice in my head say, *No more Mak. No more Mak.* Over and over, like a broken phonograph record. Mama became concerned, and after dinner I heard her talking with Father. They were whispering. Normally, I would've been suspicious, but I was too wound up to care at that point. Father left for a while, and when he came back, he brought some dishes of applesauce for us. I hadn't eaten much and gobbled it up.

I think they must've ground up one of those sleeping pills in the applesauce, because I don't even remember falling asleep that night. When I got up the next morning, I felt better, but also a little like my head was filled with old socks. I didn't like that feeling, but it was better than hearing that voice in my head singing, *No more Mak.* After breakfast I started saying to myself, *Mak'll come back. Mak'll come back.* I figured if I had to listen to a voice in my head, it might as well say something helpful. I'm not sure if it made it any more likely that Mak would return. But I did seem to cry a little less when I remembered to say it.

About two weeks later I returned to our barracks with Father after we'd gone for a walk. Mama was sitting at the table, a letter in her hands. She waved the letter when we walked in.

"Good or bad?" said Father.

Anytime we received a letter since we'd started getting those horrible telegrams about Mak, Father and Mama would always ask "Good or bad?" right away so they could prepare themselves for whatever was to come.

"Good," said Mama. "It is a letter from Eunice!"

Eunice! I felt excited just to hear her name.

"Come and sit down and I will read it," Mama said excitedly.

Father and I took our seats by the table, and Mama began to read.

"'We and a few other families are working what are

called truck farms. These are small produce farms outside of Chicago. We grow cucumbers, celery, and lots of different flowers. We lease the land and share our crops with the owner as partial payment. Once we get a harvest, we'll rent a truck and bring it to markets in the city. In the meantime, there is plenty of work: lots of factories making goods for the war—clothing, vehicles, weapons.'"

Mama looked up, smiling.

"That sounds wonderful, don't you think?" she said.

"Yes, well . . . ," said Father. "It does have promise. But I'm not sure how these little 'truck farms' would compare to the kind of farm we could get in Omaha."

"Ichiro, please, no talk about Omaha just now."

Mama and Father had come to an agreement about his fascination with Omaha. It was decided that we would work toward making a new life in Omaha if he could provide information on:

a. how we would buy land in Nebraska, and

b. how we would live and make money until we became corn farmers.

Father had yet to provide that information. It seemed his crazy need to move to Omaha had begun to fade. But not entirely.

"You know what they say in Omaha: 'The corn is as high as an elephant's eye!'" said Father.

"Ichiro, please," replied Mama.

"Alright," sighed Father.

"Thank you," said Mama, and she continued reading. "'If you send us a letter stating your desire to lease a farm and a bank draft for two hundred dollars, we can rent a five-acre plot for you right next to ours. It's not a lot of land, but there is more to be acquired as we prosper. Working together makes many things easier for all of us.'"

Father rubbed the stubble on his chin.

"I don't know, Aki. Only five acres. I am used to working a much bigger farm."

"We worked nine acres in Florin," replied Mama. "That is not 'much bigger.' And besides, Eunice says there will be more land available in time."

"Hmmm . . . ," said Father.

"And there is also this," said Mama, continuing. "'Not once have I heard "Remember Pearl Harbor!" or seen a single sign that says "No Japs Served Here." Granted, Chicago is not a perfect place. People are as frightened of Japan here as they are everywhere else in the United States. But it is much better here. Much better.'"

Mama put the letter down and looked at Father. He sighed and looked out the window. Mama stood up, put on her coat, and walked to the door.

"I am going for a walk," she said. "We can talk more about this later."

Father stood.

"I don't know much about Chicago," he said. "Except that it is famous for wind."

"I trust Eunice," said Mama. "I will be back soon. Let's sleep on it and talk more tomorrow."

For the next few days, Mama and Father bounced the idea of moving to Chicago back and forth. I wasn't included in these talks. This was frustrating but something I was used to. I did, however, very much like the idea of moving near Eunice. Since Chicago meant spending more time with Eunice, I was all for it.

For Mama, moving to Chicago made perfect sense, and whenever Father asked her to explain why she liked the idea so much, she'd just share what she'd read to us from Eunice's letter. Father didn't appear to hate the idea, but he certainly didn't love it either. He offered several reasons why we shouldn't move there: too far east, too far north, too cold, lots of snow. And, of course, there was the issue of the wind.

"I have talked to several friends and they all agree—Chicago is far too windy. Too windy to live in. And much too windy to farm in."

"The weather wasn't perfect in Florin, Ichiro," sighed Mama. "Remember? That didn't stop us from farming there."

"Ah, but this Chicago is renowned for wind," replied Father. "Some even refer to it as the Windy City! Can you imagine how windy it must be if all of the cities in the United States call Chicago *the* Windy City! Such wind!"

"Ichiro," said Mama. "We are running out of time. The camp is closing. Eunice will not wait forever for us to respond to her offer."

"I know these things, Aki."

"Eunice's offer is a good one," said Mama.

"Yes," replied Father.

And that was it.

That was the end of their going back and forth about

whether we would grow corn in Omaha or run a truck farm in Chicago. Father never said, *You're right, Aki. No more Omaha! Chicago is the place for us. Who cares how windy it is?* And nobody ever told me, *Mari—we're going to Chicago!* But that's what happened. I could've been angry about being left out of the decision, but like I said, it was something I was used to. And besides, we were going to be neighbors with Eunice! It was more fun to think about that than be angry.

The very next day we started packing. Father booked us bus tickets to Sacramento and a connection from there to Chicago by train. These tickets were part of the government's deal—each of us got a one-way ticket to anywhere in the US (east of Manzanar, of course) plus twenty-five dollars. When Father came back from the main office, he showed the tickets and the cash to Mama.

"Twenty-five dollars," she said in disgust. "Twenty-five dollars for three years in Manzanar. It is beyond insulting."

Mama wanted to burn the money, but Father wouldn't let her.

"We are not so rich that we can throw away money," he said.

He placed the envelope with the cash and tickets into his jacket's inner pocket. This was also where he kept the check for the money we'd received for the sale of our farm. That pocket held all the wealth that our family possessed.

There wasn't much to pack, so there wasn't much for me to do. Mama let me stroll around the camp and say goodbye. I spent more time saying goodbye to places—the arch I'd drawn in the Momoyama garden, the Children's Village—than to people. There was, however, one formerly friendly place that I very much chose not to say goodbye to: the camouflage factory. I didn't care if I never stood in the shadow of its billowing sheets of rotting camouflage ever again.

We ate our last meal, breakfast, in the mess hall. I looked around and thought about the food—so much of it boiled and bland, the SPAM, the cabbage, the beans. I would not miss that. But then I thought about all the faces. So many people weren't there—Oba-chan Yuki, of course; Keiko; Sydney; the Clucking Sisters (they'd left for St. Louis a few weeks earlier); the kids from school. All those faces—gone. I would miss them. Even the ones I thought I didn't like.

Of the few who were still there, many were old men. It was a sad thing to see. It meant to me that they had no family, no younger ones to take them along when they left Manzanar for an eastern city. Father got up after he'd finished his meal and made his way around the room. I watched and listened as he greeted the old men. He was gentle, respectful as he said goodbye to each of them. Later I would draw Father making his farewells.

After breakfast we made our way back to our barracks. Our things sat packed in a few suitcases and some larger boxes tied tightly with string and plastered with labels with our new address—Eunice's address—on them. The room was empty except for the metal frames that held our ratty, old, skinny mattresses. There was nothing left to show that this had been our home for almost three years.

I started to cry—just a little sniffling sort of crying at first, but soon it turned into gulping sobs. I looked around the room and remembered—that was where Mak had slept, that was where I had sat and drawn in my sketchbook, that was where all of us had sat together and sipped the tea we'd made on our heater. Mama came over and put her hand on my shoulder.

"Time to go, Mari," she said quietly.

I noticed Father was doing something over by the heater. He bent down and picked up what looked like a rock that had sat at the heater's foot. I got a look at it before he put it in his coat pocket. It was a cast-iron Buddha, about the size of an apple. I'd forgotten he put it there when we first moved in.

"Now we can leave," said Father.

We picked up our suitcases and walked out into the dusty street. The wind had picked up. *Perfect,* I thought. *Just like Manzanar to say goodbye to us with another dust storm.* Father brought out the boxes and piled them and our suitcases into a wheelbarrow he had borrowed from the garden.

With Father in the lead, we made our way out of Manzanar. A few friends sat or stood on their barracks' stoops. They waved as we passed. We waved back. A friend of Mama's came out to us as we shuffled along. She hugged Mama and gave her a wrapped gift. I heard Mama's friend say the word "scarf" and the phrase "windy city." They both laughed at this and then they cried. A friend of Father's joined him, and he accompanied us all the way out to the front gate.

A soldier stood in the stone guard post. He smiled as we walked by.

"So long," he said cheerily. "Good luck."

"Thank you. You as well" was, I think, Father's response.

The wind had picked up and garbled his reply. He'd said something, I'm just not sure exactly what it was. Mama, like me, looked straight ahead and said nothing.

We stood out by the road. In the distance I could see the fuzzy brown dot that was the bus as it made its way toward us. Mama took the scarf her friend had made for her and wrapped it around my mouth and nose. She pulled off the kerchief she'd tied about her hair and wrapped that around her own face. Father took the boxes and suitcases from the wheelbarrow. He shook his friend's hand. The man waved to Mama and me and then trotted back into the camp, pushing the wheelbarrow. The wind whipped and tugged at the dust that rose behind him.

I turned to find that our bus had arrived. The driver hopped down and placed our suitcases and boxes in a large compartment on the side, while we climbed in. I didn't notice if this bus had the painting of the odd-looking dog on its side. I was too busy getting out of the wind and into the bus before I thought to look. We took our seats, Father on one side of the aisle next to a sleeping man, and Mama and me on the other.

"They took three years from us. But we're out, Aki. We're finally out," whispered Father, leaning across the aisle toward us.

Mama remained silent, looking straight ahead. It

seemed as if she was staring at something out the front window. I tried to see it, but there was nothing there, just the road ahead. I took her hand and squeezed. Mama smiled at me, then turned her gaze back to the road in front of us.

The bus engine roared. I looked back at the camp. The windows were very dirty, but I caught a glimpse of the last gasp of a small dust tornado as it danced about the base of a guard tower and collapsed. I turned away from the window and thought about them—the tower and the little tornado.

How would I draw that? I wondered.

AUTHOR'S NOTE

I was a boy when I first began to learn about the Japanese American internment. A librarian had given me several books about children who'd lived through the Holocaust. I was overwhelmed by these stories and read them one right after the other. I remember spending lots of time talking with my mom about what I read about concentration camps and Nazi atrocities and Jewish people fighting back from the ghettos they'd been forced into. I remember wondering, *How could grown-ups treat kids like this?*

It was during one of those conversations at the kitchen table that my mother informed me that my great aunt Adeline and her daughter Mary and Mary's kids had been put in an American concentration camp during World War II. After all the reading I'd done, I imagine I must've been doubtful. I must've said *Wait. What? Hold on, Mom, we didn't build concentrations camps in America.* And that's when she told me about Adeline and Mary. How they were forced into a prison camp—the Manzanar Relocation Center. About the reason for their being imprisoned: Mary's father was Japanese. About Adeline not having to go to the camp because she was white. And about how Adeline went anyway because, c'mon, she wasn't going to let them put her kid and her grandkids in a prison camp in the desert without her being there to help them.

By that time, my mom had lost touch with my great aunt, and the story of Adeline and Mary had become a myth in my family. My mom was very proud of her aunt and cousin, their grit and dedication to each other in the face of systemic racism and outrageous abuse by our government. And so we never forgot them. However, what my mom shared with me about that terrible time in our history was more about the heroic story of Adeline and Mary than it was about the facts of the Japanese American internment.

It wasn't till later—just after 9/11, when I started to hear paranoid, racist voices in America call for new internment camps, this time for Muslims—that I realized it'd become very important that I make a book that related some of Adeline and Mary's story. And it was while I was doing research for that book, *Gaijin: American Prisoner of War* that I started to learn about the monstrous facts of the Japanese American internment.

In my research, I spoke with people who'd been imprisoned in those camps, as well as with people whose parents, grandparents, and great-grandparents had been imprisoned. I visited the sites of two internment camps in California: Tanforan and Manzanar. I read books and visited websites, lots and lots of websites, to learn all I could about the internment. And later, while making this book, I watched lots of interviews with men who'd fought in the Japanese American *Go For Broke* battalion, the 100th/442nd.

Through all that research, there are two things that continue to stand out for me. The first is the fact that half of the approximately 120,000 Japanese Americans who were removed from their homes and stuck in these remote, bleak prison camps were children. Think of it: 60,000 kids, some of them removed from orphanages, were put in prison camps in the desert, surrounded by barbed wire, housed in plywood shacks, frightened by the threat of soldiers, guns, bayonets, guard towers, etc. It sounds like the plot of a dystopian nightmare, doesn't it? But that's what we did. And it left me with the same question I asked when I was a kid: *How could grown-ups do this to kids?*

The second thing that I simply can't forget is the fact that so many of the Japanese American men who joined the 100th/442nd were fighting for the country that had put them and their families in prison camps. I am baffled by that. I can only guess that they must've believed so deeply in the promise of America that, in spite of the abuse to themselves and their families at home, they were still willing to put their lives on the line to defend that promise.

We owe so much to these Japanese American children, these women and men, these families who we put into these camps. We need to acknowledge their loss. And we need to honor the Japanese American soldiers who sacrificed so much in Europe while their families were imprisoned in America. Our country should regularly express regret for what we did. That expression won't fix the vastness of what was done to that community. But it might help. Let's learn the history of the internment and share it with others. Let's never forget what we did as a nation to Japanese Americans, so that we can help them heal and so that we may never do it again. Not ever again.

"Whatever you do will be insignificant,
but it is very important that you do it."
—Mahatma Gandhi

ACKNOWLEDGEMENTS

I am grateful. I thank my wife, Kristen Remenar, for her love and support. I thank my cousins Adeline Tirado and Anita Emily Torres for sharing the story of their lives with our beloved Obachans Adeline and Mary. I thank my editor, Reka Simonsen, for the tremendous story-crafting knowledge that she brought to the process of making this book; and I thank my art director, Michael McCartney, for the wonderful work he's done. Last but not least, I thank my agent, Abigail Samoun, for her expert help in all things publishing.

SELECTED RESOURCES BIBLIOGRAPHY

Books

Cahan, Richard, and Michael Williams. *Un-American: The Incarceration of Japanese Americans During World War II.* Chicago: CityFiles Press, 2016.

Chang, Thelma. *"I Can Never Forget": Men of the 100th/442nd.* Honolulu: Sigi Productions, 1991.

Elms, Matthew, and The American Battle Monuments Commission. *When the Akimotos Went to War: An Untold Story of Family, Patriotism and Sacrifice during World War II.* U.S. Independent Agencies and Commissions, 2015.

Ishizuka, Karen L. *Lost and Found: Reclaiming the Japanese American Incarceration.* Chicago: University of Illinois Press, 2006.

McGaugh, Scott. *Honor Before Glory: The Epic World War II Story of the Japanese American GIs Who Rescued the Lost Battalion.* Boston: Da Capo Press/Perseus Books, 2016.

Masuda, Minoru. *Letters from the 442nd: The World War II Correspondence of a Japanese American Medic.* Edited by Hana Masuda and Dianne Bridgman, with a foreword by Senator Daniel K. Inouye. Seattle: The University of Washington Press, 2008.

Muller, Eric L., ed. *Colors of Confinement: Rare Kodachrome Photographs of Japanese American Incarceration in World War II.* With photographs by Bill Manbo. Chapel Hill: University of North Carolina Press, 2012.

Reeves, Richard. *Infamy: The Shocking Story of the Japanese American Internment in World War II.* New York: Picador/Henry Holt and Co., 2015.

Websites

https://encyclopedia.densho.org

http://the442.org/home.html

https://goforbroke.org

home.nps.gov/manz/learn/historyculture/japanese-americans-at-manzanar.htm